ALIAS™

SISTER SPY

LAURA PEYTON ROBERTS

AN ORIGINAL PREQUEL NOVEL BASED ON THE
HIT TV SERIES CREATED BY J. J. ABRAMS

BANTAM BOOKS

NEW YORK ★ TORONTO ★ LONDON ★ SYDNEY ★ AUCKLAND

ALIAS: SISTER SPY

A Bantam Book / May 2003
Text and cover art copyright © 2003 by Touchstone Television

ISBN: 0-553-49401-5

Visit us on the Web! www.randomhouse.com

Published simultaneously in the United States and Canada

Bantam Books is an imprint of Random House Children's Books, a
division of Random House, Inc. BANTAM BOOKS and the rooster
colophon are registered trademarks of Random House, Inc.

PRINTED IN THE UNITED STATES OF AMERICA

OPM 10 9 8 7 6 5 4 3 2 1

Everyone was talking and shouting, trying to figure out what had happened. At the center of the biggest knot, only feet from the low side railing, Sydney spotted Ashley, babbling frantically to Roxy and two crewmen.

Her sense of foreboding growing, Sydney pushed her way through the crowd.

"That girl! You know, that *girl*!" Ashley kept repeating. "She was right here. I just saw her!"

"Who, Ashley?" Roxy looked scared. "Calm down and tell us what happened."

"A splash! You heard it, right, Roxy? You heard the splash?"

"It was a splash?" one of the crewmen said apprehensively. "What kind of splash?"

Ashley clawed desperately at Roxy's arm. Her glassy eyes rolled Sydney's way and Sydney's insides froze.

SHE WAS NO LONGER CERTAIN ASHLEY WAS FAKING ANYTHING.

Don't miss any of the
OFFICIAL ALIAS BOOKS
from Bantam Books!

Declassified: the official companion

THE PREQUEL SERIES
Recruited
A Secret Life
Disappeared
Sister Spy

And coming soon
The Pursuit / A Michael Vaughn Novel

If you think being a full-time college freshman and a part-time agent-in-training with the **CIA** is easy, you've never tried it. For one thing, my boss, Wilson, doesn't seem to fully grasp the meaning of *part-time*. My schedule is a killer. If I'm not drilling with my self-defense instructors, practicing state-of-the-art surveillance techniques, or learning *yet another* language, I'm flying all over the world.

All right. That part's pretty cool.

And I know what I'm doing is incredibly important. I **believe** in this job like I've never believed in anything else.

But just once I'd like to blow off an entire Saturday and sleep till noon on Sunday. Like a **normal** person. You know?

Oops. That's my pager. Gotta go.

"YOU WANT ME TO *what*?" Sydney Bristow asked incredulously. She shook her head, laughing with disbelief. "Good one, Wilson!"

Reginald Wilson, her SD-6 recruiter, leaned forward in his leather chair, bracing his hands on the long polished table at the center of the op-tech department. "This is serious, Sydney."

"You just told me to join a sorority! You *must* be joking. Right?"

Wilson's eyes bored into hers, not a trace of humor in them.

"Right?" she repeated, more urgently. "I mean, you can't be telling me that the future of the free world hangs on my mastery of panty raids and keg parties."

"I believe panty raids would be more of a fraternity thing," Wilson said dryly. "Or possibly sixth-grade camp. However, you *will* be required to demonstrate an affinity for crafts, formals, and soul-baring games. Obviously you have some research to do before you attend your first event at Alpha Kappa Chi."

He's kidding, she thought. *He has to be!*

But Wilson was a model secret agent—his face gave away nothing.

"I cannot join a sorority," Sydney said, doing her best to keep her voice calm. "Not unless you want to have someone hack into the school computer and fix the failing grades I'll get. I've seen those girls on campus, running around in their matching outfits. Just reading all the banners they put up would be a full-time gig—I can't imagine actually attending so many events. It's like they live in an alternate universe or something, and I just don't have time for a third reality right now. Between working for you and trying to pass my classes, I'm living two lives already."

She could have added that her impression of sororities was not particularly positive, but that objection seemed obvious. Sydney's studiousness, her reserved personality, and her outsider social status—all characteristics that had made her a prime candidate for recruitment into this top-secret branch of the CIA—were in diametric opposition to the sorority lifestyle.

"You may have a point," Wilson admitted, rubbing his square chin thoughtfully. "But a little careful hacking is certainly an option. There's this new kid in ops who—"

"Wilson!" Sydney stopped him. "I don't *want* to join a sorority. I wouldn't fit in with those girls, and don't even get me started on frat boys! I'm totally in favor of exploring the college experience, but if you're going to start filling up my free time now—"

"Who said anything about free time? I'm giving you your next mission."

"Joining a *sorority*?"

"Joining Alpha Kappa Chi," Wilson corrected her impatiently. "It wouldn't do any good if you joined one of the others."

What good will it do you if I join that one?

Taking a deep breath, Sydney forced herself to swallow the question. In fairness to Wilson, she hadn't given him much of a chance to explain. Her two most recent missions, in Paris and Scotland, had been the kind of life-or-death international spying assignments she'd joined SD-6 to perform. How did a sorority fit in to the mix?

"Why don't we start over?" she asked sheepishly.

Wilson gave her a stern look. "Try to pay attention this time."

"Right. Sorry."

Sinking lower in her chair, she hoped the two agents walking past the large conference room hadn't heard the reprimand. In the months since she'd begun her training, Sydney had earned her reputation as a nineteen-year-old wunderkind, but she still wasn't a full agent.

"As I was saying," Wilson continued in a slightly annoyed tone, "I want you to join Alpha Kappa Chi immediately. We had an agent in there, Jen Williams. Unfortunately, Jen died two weeks ago. The coroner called it an asthma attack, but we don't buy that for a second."

"Wait," said Sydney, sitting up straight. "You think somebody killed her?"

Wilson nodded. "Jen did have asthma, but it had been under control for years. Suffocation. That's my guess. With her history, people might not look too carefully."

"But . . . but . . ." Sydney tried to latch on to one of the thoughts swirling through her brain. "You think she was killed for being in a *sorority*?"

"No. I think someone in the sorority killed her."

"So . . . they knew she was an agent?"

"Why else would they have killed her?"

"It doesn't make sense," said Sydney. "Why did

you send her in there in the first place? I mean, who *are* these girls?"

Wilson massaged his temples, clearly trying to fend off a headache. "I didn't *send* her in. When we recruited Jen, she was already a member of Alpha Kappa Chi. It was difficult, working around all those functions, but it was also a built-in cover. Who's going to suspect a sorority girl?"

"Not me," Sydney admitted.

"Exactly. Plus, the Alphas are a well-off group. They travel a lot. Jen did some odd drops and pick-ups for us. Mostly little stuff, but she was about to graduate and come on as a full-time agent."

"She was a senior?" Sydney asked, wishing she could have met her. She hadn't even known there was another member of SD-6 enrolled at her school . . . and now the girl was dead.

"She started with us later than you did, and didn't move forward as fast. But Jen was a good, solid thinker. Her death is a big loss."

Sydney nodded, her eyes abruptly brimming with tears. "I'll find out who did it," she vowed. "I'll rush that sorority so hard they won't know what hit them."

Wilson smiled faintly. "There's more. AKX is gearing up for its big spring trip to Hawaii, and Jen was going to do a mission for us there—the most important mission we'd ever given her. You'll have to take it now."

"I will. Anything."

Wilson gave her a long, probing look.

"Don't make this personal," he warned. "Whoever killed Jen is still out there. You storm in like the Terminator and you could end up dead too."

"I'll be careful."

"See that you are. We want to know what happened to Jen, but not if it costs us the mission—or another agent."

The way Wilson was looking at her made her stomach knot with fear. Joining a sorority no longer seemed the least bit funny.

Sydney swallowed hard. "It could have been someone outside the sorority who killed her."

"I'm open to all possibilities. But Jen died in the AKX house, in her own bed—and that points to an inside job. Watch your back every second, Sydney. I can't stress that enough."

* * *

Walking across the sprawling Los Angeles campus on her way back to her dorm room, Sydney barely noticed the sun sinking into a smoggy red haze or the bicycles and skateboards weaving across her path. Instead, Wilson's warnings rang in her ears, and a map of southern Oahu filled her inner vision.

"The sorority will be staying in Waikiki," Wilson

had told her, pointing to the display on an op-tech monitor. "Pearl Harbor is here, a short drive away. You'll have to get most of your equipment on the island, obviously."

"Obviously," she'd echoed, still reeling.

Wilson had handed her a Global Positioning System unit, an electronic device used for finding exact locations anywhere on the globe. The gadget looked like a TV remote with a tiny square LCD screen.

"It's waterproof," he'd said. "The mission coordinates have already been entered. Make sure you know how GPS works, and whatever you do, don't lose it."

"I won't."

She reached behind her now as she walked, locating the small lump the instrument made through the fabric of her backpack.

"All right, then? Is everything clear?" he'd asked.

"Crystal," she'd responded in her most confident voice.

But now, out among normal people again, she could barely believe what she'd just learned.

A nuclear device, she thought, still stunned. *At the bottom of Pearl Harbor. All these years . . .*

"It's not a *live* device," Wilson had assured her. "It's a prototype of a unique detonation system for an atomic bomb. A sort of scale model. For years it was thought that Benjamin Suler, the only scientist working on the project, had made both himself and his work disappear. Only a handful of brass ever knew about Suler, and after Hiroshima they decided finding the prototype was irrelevant. They were wrong. We've had a researcher on this full-time ever since we heard about it, trying to track that device down."

"Why?" she had asked, but she was already starting to see the possibilities.

"It's a dangerous world we live in, Sydney. And while technology has moved on since the A-bomb, it's believed the detonation system Suler developed would have made a more deadly bomb than the ones we eventually dropped on Japan. Smaller, more efficient. More powerful."

"*More* powerful?" she'd repeated, her mind replaying the footage she'd seen of the mushroom cloud over Hiroshima. The devastation that bomb had caused was wrenching to consider. To think that it could have been *worse* . . .

"Let's just say we don't want this prototype falling into the wrong hands. The technology may be crude by today's standards, but that's its appeal—it's simple to make. At best, it would cost a staggering amount of money to get the thing back. At worst . . ."

"We wouldn't get it back," she'd finished for him, imagining nuclear bombs stashed in the hideouts of terrorists and warlords throughout the world.

For just a moment fear had flickered behind Wilson's impassive features. Then the crack in his mask had sealed and he smiled again. "The good news is, we found it first. And right under our noses. Kind of ironic, really."

Ironic, Sydney thought now, reaching the main entrance to her dorm. She climbed the stairs in a trance, her mind still sifting through the chaos of a long-ago war.

When the Japanese had launched their sneak attack on Pearl Harbor that Sunday morning in 1941, their pilots had killed thousands of U.S. servicemen and sunk ships of all descriptions. Both American and Japanese aircraft had crashed during the fierce battle, and when the carnage was over, the surface of the harbor had burned in a horrifying stew of floating fuel and body parts.

During the long war that followed, the ruined military hardware that came to rest at the bottom of the murky green harbor was never fully catalogued. Years later, a memorial was built over the rusting hull of the sunken battleship *Arizona*. The equally enormous *Utah* still lay on its side nearby. But numerous other ships, planes, and Japanese subs had sunk, and though most were eventually recovered, surprises had been discovered over the years as the tangled story of that morning continued to unravel.

"When I first heard, I couldn't believe it," Wilson had told her. "Right there in the harbor. All this time . . ."

According to Wilson's research, Dr. Benjamin Leonard Suler had been secretly visiting a colleague aboard a yacht in Pearl Harbor when the Japanese had attacked. Suler's body was now presumed to have been among the hundreds never identified. The fate of the prototype was another story.

"He took it everywhere he went, in a specially built stainless-steel case. He was obsessive like that. Paranoid." Sydney could still see Wilson's eyes burning with intensity. "When the fighting started, he would have been consumed with saving his work, hiding it from the enemy. It's on that boat. It has to be."

And the boat, the *Eagle,* was at the bottom of Pearl Harbor. At least that was Wilson's theory, now that new top-secret remote sensing techniques had picked up a previously undetected mass in forty feet of water. All she had to do was sneak onto a military base under cover of darkness, dive to a wreck no one had ever seen, and find a lunchbox-sized case hidden by a paranoid lunatic.

Piece of cake, she thought sarcastically, reaching for the door to her room and opening it with one quick shove.

"You're back!" her best friend and roommate, Francie Calfo, exclaimed, scrambling up from the papers spread out on her twin bed. She was wearing old sweats and a tank top, her black hair wound into a knot secured by a pencil on top of her head. "Please, *please,* distract me from all this studying!"

Sydney smiled, brought back to earth by her friend's urgent plea. "It *is* Friday," she offered. "You have the entire weekend to finish whatever you're doing."

"That's the stuff," Francie encouraged, raising her brows. "Give me more."

Sydney thought a moment. "I've decided to join a sorority."

"Get *out!*" Francie squealed, rushing forward. "No, wait," she said, stopping abruptly. "You're just yanking me. Right?"

"No, I'm totally serious. I mean, I realize I'm not the most sociable person . . . but being in a sorority isn't like hanging out with strangers. You get to know all those girls really well. Don't you think it would be fun?"

"But—but—" Francie sputtered, too astonished to form a sentence. "You don't *like* doing stuff like that. I have to drag you to frat parties."

"True," Sydney admitted. "But I'm not joining a fraternity."

"It's all the same," Francie insisted. "I mean, I'm not trying to talk you out of it. But . . . why the sudden change of heart?"

Sydney played with a strand of her brown hair, searching for a believable answer. "I guess I'm kind of bored," she said at last. "Of me, I mean. All I ever do is work, and study, and work. This is college, the time of our lives, and I feel like I'm missing it. I don't want to look back and kick myself for the things I could have done. It's time to take drastic action."

"Well . . . congratulations," said Francie. "If you're looking for drastic, you've found it."

"You think I'm crazy."

"Not crazy. Just . . ." Francie shook her head. Then, finally, she smiled. "You're really serious?"

"I am."

"Okay, then. You'd better mean it, because I'm joining with you."

Sydney stifled a groan, knowing she should have expected that. Francie was far more outgoing than she was, striking up conversations with everyone from the cute boy on the next floor to total strangers in the lunch line. She loved parties and was usually first on the dance floor, even if it meant grabbing some random guy for her partner. Francie had never been seen at a social event with her back pressed into a corner and a plastic cup clutched in front of her, Sydney's favorite defensive position. Francie was sorority material all the way.

"We'll have to research the houses," Francie announced, sitting down at her desk and hitting the Power button on her laptop. "I mean, I already pretty much know them, but this is a *huge* decision.

Every sorority has its own personality. We want to find the group that's exactly perfect for us."

"I've already picked one." Shrugging off her backpack, Sydney dropped it on her bed, pretending not to notice Francie's amazed stare.

"Just like that?" Francie demanded. "Forget about rush, I'm not even logged on yet! You have to at least check out their Web sites!"

"I'm joining Alpha Kappa Chi."

For a moment, Francie was literally shocked into silence. Then she burst out laughing.

"Sure you are," she said. "You've decided to quit working at the bank and rob it instead."

SD-6 hid its existence by posing as a bank, Credit Dauphine, to outsiders. Francie believed Sydney's part-time job there was as a lowly clerk, but that still didn't explain why she thought Sydney needed to rob her employer.

"What are you talking about?" Sydney asked, stripping off the button-down shirt she'd worn to work. Her khakis came off next, leaving her talking in her bra and underwear.

"Those girls are rich! AKX—are you kidding me? The other Greeks call them the Trust Fund Club."

"Well, what difference does it make? They're not going to keep me out just because I don't vacation on Saint Bart's."

"Don't bet on it," Francie said darkly, typing

away at her computer. Suddenly her face brightened. "Here are some girls we ought to be looking at— Sigma Omega. A couple of them are in my biology class, and they're really nice. They do a lot of community service, too. Remember those bins all over campus for collecting aluminum cans? They use the cash to buy books for a children's shelter."

"That is nice," Sydney conceded, wrapping a bath towel around her middle. "But my mind's already made up."

"Just tell me this: Why AKX?"

"I . . . like their house."

She knew how shallow she sounded, but it was the best she could do just then. If the girls were as rich as Francie claimed, it seemed likely they'd have a nice house. She half expected her friend to throw up her hands in disgust, but to her surprise Francie smiled.

"They *do* have the best house. And I've heard there's an even more incredible pool behind it."

"So it's settled, then," Sydney said, relieved. "AKX, here we come."

She started to head for the shower.

"It's not that easy, Syd. First they have to let us in."

"Yeah." Sydney stopped and turned back to face her friend. "What's the deal with that, anyway? Do you know how we join?"

"Well, rush is in the fall. Everyone who wants to—"

"No. How do we join *today*?"

Francie rocked back, surprised. "I don't think we can."

"There has to be a way." Sydney gestured to the computer. "If you see what you can find out there, as soon as I get out of the shower I'll—"

A loud rap on their door cut Sydney off in mid-sentence.

"Who's that?" Sydney asked.

"You're closer," Francie said, not moving.

Sydney walked to the door and pulled it open, expecting to find one of the other girls on their floor. Instead, Burke Wells stood in the hallway, a sweet, expectant smile on his face and a cellophane-wrapped bunch of daisies in one hand.

"Burke!" she exclaimed, slamming the door. Blood rushed to her cheeks as Francie's amused laughter rang out behind her.

"This isn't funny!" she hissed at her friend, frantically rewrapping her towel in an attempt to get more coverage.

"Au contraire," Francie said, laughing. "What's he doing here?"

Sydney reopened the door slightly and peered out through the crack. Burke's expectant expression was gone, but his smile was even broader.

"You don't look ready," he observed. "Although, to tell the truth, that towel thing is working for me."

He shrugged, his shaggy red hair brushing his shoulders. "What the heck? I'm ready to set a new trend if you are."

"It's just that I worked later than expected. Then I started talking to my roommate and I . . . I totally lost track of time."

She didn't have the heart to tell him that she'd also completely forgotten they were supposed to go out that night.

"I'm so sorry, Burke. But I really have to shower. If you could maybe wait . . . or go do something else and come back . . ."

She wouldn't have blamed him for being mad, but Burke just handed her the daisies.

"Here," he said with an easy grin. "Put these in water too."

* * *

"So, where are we going?" Sydney asked as she and Burke stepped out of her dorm into the soft, warm air of a late-spring evening. She had dried and dressed so quickly that evaporation still prickled behind her ears, and her damp ponytail switched coolly between her bare shoulders.

"Me? I'm in charge now?" he asked, surprised. "You're the one who asked me out for pizza."

"Right. I did."

And she had chosen her venue carefully. Pizza was the ultimate date with training wheels, a chance for her and Burke to get to know each other without the raised expectations of a more romantic setting. If she'd been choosing a restaurant to eat at with Noah, on the other hand . . .

Don't think about Noah Hicks, she ordered herself automatically. *If Noah weren't such a cold, noncommittal jerk, you'd have never called Burke in the first place.*

Not that Noah cares.

The thought made her glance guiltily at her date. Burke was so nice, so laid back, so . . . *normal.* She hated even to think she might be using him to get back at Noah.

"What do you like on your pizza?" she asked, impulsively grabbing Burke's hand. "I have this whole theory about divining people's personalities through their favorite pizza toppings."

"Sorry to disappoint you," he said, "but I like just about everything."

"That doesn't disappoint me. In fact, it practically proves I'm on to something."

"It does, huh?" He pulled her closer, his shoulder rubbing against hers. "Do you think I'm easy now?"

Her pulse raced, as much from the sudden contact as from the question. She could smell the spice coming off his skin—cologne, maybe, or some exotic soap from one of those all-natural stores he frequented. The perpetual stubble on his chin ruled out aftershave. His gorgeous hazel eyes gazed into hers, so clear, so direct, so open. . . .

"I don't know *what* to think about you," she teased, trying to break the intensity of the moment. "Judging by your politics, there's a pretty good chance you're crazy, but I'll try to keep an open mind."

"I'm going to convert you. Wait and see. Once you sink your teeth into your first good conspiracy, you never go back."

"I'll have to take your word for that."

So far Burke had failed to convince her that the *Challenger* space shuttle disaster had been the result of sabotage, or that splinter militias within the military were plotting to overthrow the U.S. government, or even that the school commons was controlling student behavior through an unhealthy, hormone-laced diet. He was cute when he got worked up, though.

She gave him another sideways glance.

Adorable, she decided.

The pizza restaurant on the edge of campus was jammed to its low, dark rafters. They had to wait for a table, then wait even longer for the vegetarian pizza that eventually arrived. Sydney braced herself for that awkward pause in conversation, the one where they suddenly realized they had run out of things to say to each other, but it never arrived.

She was starting to suspect that Burke never ran out of things to say.

"So, tell me about your job at the bank," he directed, helping himself to a second slice. The melted cheese stretched into threads that caught in the stubble on his chin. He wiped his face with his hand, completely unself-conscious.

"There isn't much to tell," she replied. "It's just a job. You know."

"But what do you *do* there? Typing? Filing?" He winked conspiratorially. "Or do they send you down to the vault and make you count all the money?"

"Yeah. That's it," she said, smiling. "Actually, they have me down there spinning straw into gold."

"I've heard that about those foreign banks," he said with a wise nod. "They're all stockpiling gold in order to undermine our currency and throw America into chaos."

Sydney snorted with laughter. "Okay, I've decided. You are *definitely* crazy."

"In a good way, I hope." He winked again, his changeable eyes almost green in the candlelight. His face was already so familiar she felt like they'd been friends forever.

"For a lunatic, you're all right."

"You'll come visit me in the asylum then?"

"I'll try to work it in."

They went for ice cream after dinner. The campus grounds were nearly deserted by the time Burke walked her back to her dorm.

"You don't have to come up," Sydney said, stopping outside her ground-floor lobby. "Save yourself some stairs."

"I don't mind."

"Francie will be asleep. I'd rather say good-bye here."

"You're not just trying to get out of kissing me?"

Her jaw dropped. Burke's relentless honesty was completely outside her experience. On top of that, he was right.

"No. It's just—I mean—we don't know each other that well," she stammered awkwardly. "I *like* you, but—"

"Good enough," he interrupted, wrapping his arms around her. "No tongue. I promise."

The next moment his lips were on hers, soft and warm and easy. She relaxed against him, relieved. It was a strangely friendly first kiss, unhurried . . . comfortable. No sparks, maybe, but no pressure, either.

Not like that time I kissed Noah in Paris.

The memory made her break away. She met Burke's puzzled look with an embarrassed shrug.

"I had a great time," she said. "But I really have to go up now."

"Will I see you again?" he asked anxiously.

"Of course! Definitely."

But all the way upstairs, she could only think about Noah. SD-6 Agent Hicks was every bad thing Burke wasn't: impatient, arrogant, hot-tempered.

Older, ambitious, intense. Secretive.

Mysterious.

Sydney's heart had backflipped the first time she'd seen him, and even though they'd bickered through most of their Paris mission, the connection between them had been so obvious it seemed pointless to deny it.

Meanwhile, that's obviously his plan.

Ever since they'd returned from France, Noah had been a different person. She hadn't expected him to run into her arms—not at work, anyway—but she hadn't expected him to act like he barely knew her either. Worse, he had tried to talk Wilson out of sending her to Scotland, implying she couldn't handle that mission on her own. Just remembering his unsupportive maneuvering made her blood pressure climb a notch. His behavior had been nearly as infuriating as his self-righteous expression.

I'd like to kiss that smug look right off his face.

She could do it too. Assuming she still wanted to.

Who am I kidding? she thought, sighing as she let herself into her darkened dorm room. *I'd kiss Noah again in a heartbeat.*

That was the most annoying thing of all.

Francie was asleep, her body a long lump under the blankets. Quietly closing the door, Sydney switched on her tiny desk lamp, angling it away from her friend. The beam spilled across her bed, illuminating half a ream of paper strewn about on her bedspread. She picked up the nearest sheet.

RUSH KAPPA KAPPA MU! it proclaimed in fancy letters, followed by more details than Sydney cared to know. She dropped it onto the floor, picking up a stapled stack in its place—an exhaustive history of Sigma Omega.

Something tells me Francie isn't totally on board with AKX after all.

Sydney sighed as she pushed the rest of the papers onto the floor. Switching out the light, she crawled between her sheets and pulled the blanket up over her head.

Sororities! Dealing with a nuclear bomb will be the easy part.

2

"I CAN'T BELIEVE WE'RE really here," Francie whispered excitedly to Sydney. "It's all happening so fast!"

"Fast is good." Sydney tried to sound confident as she stared up the winding brick walkway at the front of the huge Alpha Kappa Chi sorority house, but she felt like a small-town girl crashing a celebrity party. The historic two-story looked more like a Spanish mission than a residence, with rounded stucco columns fronting a deep veranda across its white façade, and wisteria-covered trellises raining lavender petals down on the lush lawn. Sydney flicked some lint off her strapless black dress and checked her nylons for runs. "I'm ready if you are."

"As ready as I'll ever be," Francie murmured weakly.

Sydney raised her chin and led the way.

In the three days since Wilson had revealed her new task, she'd done her research on sororities. Rush happened only in the fall at UCLA, but something called continuous open bidding went on at various times all year. At these smaller events a sorority might pick up a couple of pledges. And it just so happened—or had Wilson timed it?—that Alpha Kappa Chi was having its last open event of the year that Monday evening.

The house's massive front doors stood open, framing the vaulted, candlelit entry with its floor of octagonal terra-cotta tiles. An intricate black iron railing wrapped the curving wooden staircase to the right, while through the huge picture windows ahead Sydney could see the elaborate pool and surrounding backyard, landscaped and lit like a shot on a magazine cover.

"Whoa." The exclamation slipped out despite her previous decision to present a cool, slightly bored exterior.

"You're not kidding," breathed Francie.

"Listen, Francie," Sydney whispered. "The key here is to look like we're already in. We don't need these girls—we *are* these girls. So if I say something a little . . . fictional, just play along, okay? It's all part of my entrance strategy."

"Your *what*?" Francie asked, laughing nervously.

Before Sydney could elaborate, a gorgeous redhead appeared at the top of the stairs, her thick, wavy hair falling to the waistband of her faded hip-hugger jeans. A short pink T-shirt exposed a long, lean expanse of pale midriff and emphasized the sky blue jewel hovering above her pierced navel. Her toenails were painted blue too, Sydney noticed, feeling absurdly overdressed as the girl padded down to meet them.

"Hi, I'm Roxy," the redhead offered as her bare feet hit the tiles. She extended a slender hand with silver rings on every finger. "Welcome to Alpha Kappa Chi."

"Nice to meet you," Sydney got out, stunned, but determined not to lose such a golden opportunity. The names of the AKX officers were posted on their Web site—and Roxy Sinclair was president.

"I'm Sydney," she added quickly, pumping the hand Roxy offered. "And this is my friend Francie."

Roxy shook Francie's hand while Sydney tried to collect her wits. Her research had confirmed everything Francie had said about AKX's snooty reputation, and the invitation for the continuous open bidding party that night had specified cocktail attire. The last thing Sydney had expected was that the leader of these infamous snobs would turn up wearing jeans and a navel ring.

She kind of liked her for that.

"It's the clothes, right?" Roxy asked her, reading her mind. She smiled, a slight shake of her head setting her thick hair in motion. "I know, I know. If we're going to make you guys dress up, we ought to do the same. But the truth is, cocktail attire isn't my idea of a good time. Especially when the strongest cocktail we're serving tonight is cranberry juice and club soda."

"I guess you won't have any trouble separating the wannabes from the actives," Francie said uneasily, glancing down at her slinky red halter dress and matching heels.

"Don't worry about sticking out," Roxy reassured her quickly. "Most of the other sisters will dress up." She arched a perfect auburn brow. "Some of them will dress up *plenty.*"

Sydney caught the sarcasm and found herself returning Roxy's smile. The sorority's president was aware of its reputation, then. And not *all* of the girls in the house were snobs.

"Let me introduce you to a few people," Roxy offered. "Everyone's in back."

She led the way through a formal white living room dominated by a massive fireplace, cut through a cafeteria-sized kitchen, and entered a recreation room packed with plush furniture in the official sorority colors of lavender and pink. Three sets of French doors were open to the backyard, and in front of them stood an assortment of girls in their best dresses. Sydney picked out the would-be pledges easily; they were the ones holding fizzy pink drinks in clear plastic cups and trying unsuccessfully not to look stiff and nervous. Her attention immediately wandered from them to the actives, assessing each one as she tried to guess who might know something about Jen Williams's death.

"This is Keisha," Roxy said, gravitating toward a striking girl with short black hair and large dark eyes. "She's one of the good ones," she stage-whispered to Sydney. "Keisha, this is Sydney and . . . I'm sorry. What's your name again?"

"Francie," Francie supplied, her smile a tiny bit strained.

"Right. Francie." Roxy gave a cute, apologetic shrug, wrinkling her perfect nose. For a redhead, her complexion was surprisingly free of freckles.

"How's it going?" Keisha asked in a bored voice, not looking directly at them. "Roxy, what's the deal with the food tonight? I thought Ashley was in charge of catering, and she's not even here."

Roxy glanced around the room, then smiled mischievously. "I could always call for pizza."

"Oh!" exclaimed Keisha, perking up. "Would

that ever frost her! Can you imagine? A dozen Mega Meat Busters scattered around in greasy cardboard boxes? I'd whip out my credit card for that."

"You'd have to get in line." Roxy glanced at a large wall clock. "Give her fifteen more minutes, and then I'll start worrying."

"Who's your caterer?" Sydney asked, trying to break out of the background.

Keisha's eyes rested on a point above Sydney's forehead. "We use different people. Ashley's obsessed with French—she probably called Le Petit Gourmet."

"I use Marcel's for French." Sydney turned her back toward Francie, the better to ignore her friend's amazed expression. "Of course, I haven't been planning many dinners since my father remarried—*again*. Evil stepmother. You know the drill."

Keisha's smile dawned slowly, catching her face by surprise. "I *do* know the drill," she said, her gaze finally connecting with Sydney's.

"We'll all have to sit down and swap trophy-wife stories someday." Roxy rolled her blue eyes. "I bet I'll win."

A sudden commotion at the entrance to the kitchen caught everyone's attention. A tall, lanky blonde in pink silk preceded two tuxedo-clad waiters into the rec room, motioning frantically for them to begin serving appetizers from the trays balanced on their arms.

"Oh, look," said Roxy. "Here's Ashley *and* the food. I'd better go make sure there aren't any problems."

Roxy left to talk to Ashley, and when Sydney turned back to Keisha, she discovered that the other girl had slipped off too.

"What was *that*?" Francie demanded. "Your dad remarried? *Again?* What made you say such a thing?"

Sydney shrugged. She knew the role she wanted to play for these girls, but Francie knew the truth: Mr. Bristow had never remarried after his wife died in an accident when Sydney was only six. Sydney rarely spoke of her mother's death; it still hurt too much, for one thing, and the way her businessman father had neglected her since was almost as hard to accept. Besides, she was looking for common ground with these girls, not sympathy. If she had to bend the truth a bit to fit in, it was all part of the job. It was almost scary, really, how quickly she'd learned to accept that. The stories she made up for work barely even seemed like lies to her anymore. They were a cover, a strategy, a plan. . . .

Having Francie hanging around was definitely going to cramp her style.

"I mean, I know the guy has his faults," Francie continued. "But—"

"I'm trying to blend in. Okay?" Sydney cut her off in a low voice. "Do you want them to like us or not?"

"I just don't understand why you'd lie."

Keisha was wearing a diamond solitaire on her right hand. Sydney had noticed it immediately, guessed where it had come from, and taken a shot. But she couldn't explain that to Francie. She'd sound like a . . . spy.

"I don't know," Sydney said with a sigh. She made her expression as contrite as she could. "Don't pay any attention to me, okay? This whole thing is making me crazy. I just want to get in."

"But if you have to pretend to be someone you aren't . . ."

"I'm not. I won't." Sydney turned on her brightest smile. "Just a momentary lapse of sanity. Let's go meet some other people."

Francie obviously had more to say, but she dropped it. Even so, as the two of them walked into the thicker part of the crowd, Sydney decided against mentioning Jen that evening. She had memorized the girl's SD-6 file and knew enough about her now to pass herself off as a friend. People who thought she'd known Jen were more likely to give up details regarding Jen's death, but she needed to be careful about how she approached them—and about who overheard. The last thing she needed was Francie giving her the third degree for never having mentioned Jen before.

"Ooh! Stuffed mushrooms!" a girl in a white

dress cooed as a waiter passed by with a tray. "Don't you just love these?" she asked, grabbing two and turning to Francie.

Sydney sized her up: *Wannabe,* she decided.

"I haven't tried them," Francie answered.

"Oh, you have to!" the girl said, but the waiter had moved on. She shoved her napkin toward Francie, the hors d'oeuvres balanced on top. "Go ahead. Take one."

Francie hesitated, then politely accepted a mushroom. Her new friend bit into the other, releasing a gush of brown juice that cascaded off her chin and landed on the bodice of her dress. The small stain stood out like neon against the white fabric, prompting a horrified squeal from its owner.

"Oh, no! How embarrassing!" she cried, making things worse by scrubbing the spot with her pink paper napkin.

"Maybe we can find some club soda," Francie said kindly, stopping the girl's hand. "And a bathroom with a blow dryer. I can probably fix that for you."

"Really?" The girl's eyes filled with gratitude. "I'm Tina, by the way. It's really nice to meet you."

"I'm Francie. Back in a minute," she told Sydney, leading Tina off.

"The only tragedy there," a bored voice said at Sydney's ear, "is that the stain will probably come out. Did you see that Kmart dress? Polyester all the way."

Sydney turned to find herself facing Ashley, a spotless, creaseless vision in designer silk. Her glossed lips curled a bit, afflicted by the mere mention of polyester.

"Someone ought to tell her about blends. Or bibs," Sydney cracked cattily, taking her lead from Ashley.

"The red dress isn't bad," Ashley offered, watching Francie walk away. "Is she a friend of yours?"

"We're roommates," Sydney said, instinctively playing down the connection. "My name is Sydney, by the way. You're Ashley, right? The food is fabulous!"

Ashley smiled smugly. "It is, isn't it?"

Sydney was dying to point out that it was also late, just to take Miss Stuck-up down a peg, but that wouldn't get her anywhere.

"How long have you been in AKX?" she asked instead. "Are you a senior?"

"Sophomore," Ashley replied, clearly flattered. "I rushed freshman year. The *real* rush, where there's competition—not this pathetic charade. No offense," she added unconvincingly, her haughty drawl completing the caricature of a Beverly Hills socialite.

"None taken," Sydney said smoothly. "Of course I would rather have rushed in the fall. But my grandmother was in the hospital then. It looked like she wasn't going to make it."

"Well, there's always next year." Ashley smiled a bit vindictively. "We almost never take anyone from these things. So many hopefuls, so few spots . . . It's not like we're lacking for pledges."

"But you lost a girl recently, didn't you? Poor Jen. I couldn't believe it when I heard; it just seems impossible. Did she have trouble breathing often? I thought her asthma was under control."

Ashley started noticeably. "You knew Jen?"

"Our parents were friendly a few years back. We went to different high schools, though, so I didn't know her as well as I would have liked."

"I didn't know her well either," said Ashley. "I mean, we have a lot of members. I have to check on the food."

She moved off in a hurry, leaving Sydney wondering whether to follow. Ashley's strange reaction told her she was on to something. On the other hand, if she pushed too hard too early . . .

"Can I have everyone's attention?" Roxy had climbed onto an ottoman, her bare toes curling over its padded edge. "I'm Roxy Sinclair, sorority president. I want to welcome you all and thank you for coming tonight."

She paused, and in the overly enthusiastic applause that followed, Francie found her way back to Sydney.

"What did I miss?" she asked worriedly.

"Not a thing," Sydney assured her.

"We have some chairs set up in the meeting room next door," Roxy continued, pointing. "If everyone would go in there and take a seat, we have a presentation for you. A *short* presentation," she added hurriedly, as if to cushion the blow. "It won't be boring. I promise."

Far from seeming reluctant, the girls practically stormed the meeting room, a bare, low-ceilinged space with white folding chairs, where the only decorations were hand-painted pink and lavender banners. ALPHAS RULE! claimed one, while another advertised ALPHA SPIRIT! Sydney imagined the sisters in their pajamas, cranking them out the night before.

"Let's sit here, where we can see the board," Francie whispered, indicating two folding chairs near the front. A few feet away, a blank dry-erase board gave the room focus.

"I won't take a lot of your time," Roxy said, picking up a marker. Her long hair brushed her back as she wrote ALPHA KAPPA CHI—AKX in big purple letters at the top of the board. "I could tell you who we are, but if you're here, you probably already know that."

Her pronouncement was greeted by nervous giggles. She had obviously hit the mark.

"Our charter goes back to 1942, and if you like

ancient history, we have handouts in back. I'll be honest and tell you now that we rarely pick up pledges at these events. As you can see by looking around you, demand is great and our house is small." She laughed. "Relatively speaking."

Francie nudged Sydney's knee as if to say "I told you so."

"The main reason we've welcomed everyone here tonight is to give you a chance to meet the sisters and see the house, so you'll know if you're interested in rushing us next fall. But in case you're lucky enough to be offered a bid, you need to know about our upcoming event, the Alpha Aloha, which starts this Saturday. Kira?"

Another blonde made her way up to the board, this one cheerleader perky.

"The Alpha Aloha is going to be totally awesome this year!" she announced, bouncing on her toes. "Our reservations are confirmed for the Waikiki Princess, a brand-new hotel on the beach. The rooms are great, and the luau is going to be awesome—traditional roast pig, and those hunky guys in loincloths."

Approving catcalls sounded, but Kira barely stopped for breath.

"The pool is awesome, and the spa is *awesome*. Those sisters who haven't already turned in their money, you need to do it right now, because two thousand bucks is a bargain for all the fun stuff we'll be doing!"

"Thanks, Kira," said Roxy, taking over again. "Sounds . . . awesome."

Snickers sounded throughout the room, but Roxy's impish smile soothed away any sting. Even Kira laughed.

"The entire sorority goes on the Aloha," Roxy told the group. "So anyone invited to pledge would obviously attend as well. That means paying your own way. I know a week isn't much notice, but then again, it's not a lot of money."

From the corner of her eye, Sydney saw Francie stiffen.

"So, that's it, then!" Roxy concluded. "Be sure to sign our guest book with a number where we can reach you, then I hope you'll all stay for dessert. If you have any questions about the sorority, just ask one of the sisters."

"*I* have a question," Francie muttered as she and Sydney stood up. "Where are you and I going to get two thousand dollars?"

*   *   *

"What if they don't call us?" Francie worried as she and Sydney walked back across campus to their dorm. "What if they *do*? I don't have that kind of money saved, and I'm not going to pick it up in this week's waitressing tips."

"Relax," said Sydney, preoccupied with the exact same thing. The money wasn't a problem for her— SD-6 would cover that. But if she didn't get called to join, finding out what happened to Jen would be a lot more complicated. "We probably won't even get a bid."

"Oh, *that* makes me feel better."

"I don't know what you're so stressed out about. You didn't want to join AKX in the first place."

"That's true," Francie admitted, plucking at the front of her red dress. "But now I kind of do."

"Kind of?"

"All right, I do. A few of those girls, like Ashley, were exactly what I expected. But most of them are nice. And that pool! Besides, it's not like I don't *want* to go to Hawaii."

"That would be great," said Sydney, trying to stay cool. If she didn't get into AKX, Wilson could still send her to Pearl Harbor. She'd just have to investigate Jen's death another way.

"How are you going to pay for it?" Francie asked.

"What? Oh. The trip? I, uh . . . I've saved a little money from working at the bank."

"Lucky you," Francie said glumly. "I guess I could call my folks, but I can't see them agreeing that this is an emergency."

"Maybe I could loan you a few bucks."

Francie brightened. "Really? Of course, that's assuming we even get invited. How many girls do you think they'll ask?"

"Not many. Two. Maybe three. Maybe none."

"Won't it be awful if they ask one of us and not the other?" Francie stopped in her tracks, horrified by the thought. "If they don't ask us both, I won't join!"

"What? No! You definitely should."

If Francie was a member, Sydney would still have an excuse for hanging around the sorority house, poking into things. In a way, that would be even better than joining herself—all of the access with none of the obligations.

"It wouldn't be right," Francie insisted. "I mean, if they invited you and not me, you'd turn them down too. Right?"

Sydney hesitated a split second too long.

"Right?" Francie repeated.

"Why are we making up rules about stuff that will probably never happen?" Sydney finally asked. "Can't we just wait and see?"

Francie took a deep breath and started walking again. "You're right. I don't know why I'm getting so crazed. I mean, if they don't take us, there are plenty of other choices. Plus, we can rush *all* the houses in the fall."

Great, Sydney thought, forcing a smile. *What have I gotten myself into?*

* * *

The girls reached their locked dorm room door just as the telephone started ringing on the other side.

"Ooh, I'll bet it's Burke," Francie teased. "He can't endure another day without you."

"Sure. That's it," Sydney replied, trying to sound bored but digging frantically for her keys. She had waved to Burke in class that day, but they hadn't talked since their date on Friday. Flinging the door open, she launched herself across her bed and grabbed the phone off the nightstand. "Hello?"

"Hello? Sydney?" a laughing voice said on the other end. "Let me guess—you thought I was a guy."

"R-Roxy?" Sydney stammered.

"Yeah, hi. Listen, I've talked to some of the girls, and we're inviting you to pledge!"

"Already? That's . . . that's fantastic."

"Are you sure? You sound kind of stunned."

"It's just so sudden. I thought there'd be some sort of bid ceremony or something."

"We do all that ritual stuff in the fall. But if a phone call's too anticlimactic, I suppose I could break out one of the pink robes and come over there with a long-stemmed rose. . . ."

"No. No, that's not necessary," Sydney said quickly.

"Good. Because here's your first deep dark sorority secret—getting those stupid robes dry-cleaned is a real pain in the butt."

"I'll try to remember that," Sydney said, laughing. "So what's next? What's the next step?"

"If this were rush we'd send you on a scavenger hunt in your underwear, but hazing's a lot of work for only two people. Besides, we're kind of above that stuff now. Let's start with the Aloha send-off party Wednesday night. Our bros in Triple Chi are barbecuing at their place. I can't promise edible food, but they aren't too hard on the eyes."

"Sounds great," Sydney lied. "What time should we be there?"

There was a slight pause on the other end. "We?"

"Francie and I."

"Oh. Oh, right. I forgot you two were roommates." Another awkward pause. "The thing is, we're only inviting two girls, and . . . I was only calling for you."

Sydney stifled a groan. There was no question that keeping Francie out of the sorority would make things easier for her. She'd be able to say and do whatever she needed to with no one peering over her shoulder.

But Francie would be devastated. Even now she

hovered eagerly at Sydney's elbow, her dark eyes wide with hope.

"I understand," Sydney said slowly, trapped. "There's just one thing: What time should Francie and I be there?"

"She's standing right there, isn't she?" Roxy guessed.

"Exactly."

"I didn't mean to make problems for you. It's just . . . Francie doesn't fit in the way you do. She didn't speak to as many people, or at least to the right ones. She seemed a little shy."

"Shy? No way!" Sydney exclaimed. "She's twice as social as I am."

Roxy sighed. "This is going to be a problem for you, isn't it?"

"You have no idea."

"Then . . . what the heck? Bring her along." Roxy laughed, as if surprised by her own boldness. "I'm not only the president, I'm graduating this year! What are they going to do to me?"

"So . . . we both have bids?"

"I ought to be able to swing that. See you Wednesday night!"

3

"ARE YOU *POSITIVE* ROXY meant for me to
pledge too?" Francie demanded, following Sydney
through the rickety open gate into the front yard of
the fraternity house. Strings of Christmas lights in
the fraternity colors of orange and blue were draped
inside the high wooden fence, with additional illumination provided by flaming tiki torches ham-
mered into the dry, patchy grass.

"How many times do I have to say it?" Sydney
replied. "I just happened to answer the phone first."

But Francie had overheard enough of Sydney's
conversation with Roxy to be suspicious, and nothing Sydney had said in the two days since had fully

eased her mind. A last-minute invitation to drop by the sorority house that afternoon had turned into a tense experience.

"I just . . . got a weird vibe off a couple of the girls," Francie whispered, tugging nervously at the hem of her tight new pink T-shirt. AKX PLEDGE was spelled out in rhinestones across its front, the little gems reflecting blue and orange flashes from the party lights.

Sydney gestured to her own matching shirt, then across the yard to the gathering crowd. "They make us wear these goofy things in public, and you're worried about vibes? Francie, *please* forget whatever you think you heard and try to have fun, all right? You're pledging the most exclusive sorority at school, you're at a party, and everyone here is going to love you as much as I do."

Francie gave Sydney a startled look. Then, gradually, she smiled.

"The *guys* are going to love me," she conceded, her old self-confidence back. "By the time I get done here tonight, the girls will want to *be* me."

"That's the spirit."

Francie twisted a loose black curl into a perfect spiral that grazed her cheek. "If you don't mind, I think I'll cruise by myself for a while. There are a lot of people I need to talk to."

"Go ahead," Sydney urged, excited by the unexpected opportunity to talk to some people on her own.

"Catch you later." With a toss of her head, Francie headed directly for the center of the action. "Shy, my foot," she muttered as she walked away. "I'll show them shy!"

For a moment, Sydney felt guilty, knowing she'd eventually drop out of AKX and leave Francie on her own. On the other hand, Wilson hadn't exactly said when that might happen; by then Francie would probably have a bunch of new sorority friends and barely miss her at all. The realization gave Sydney a jealous pang, but she forced the thought from her mind, determined to concentrate on her mission. She wanted to question as many of the sisters as she could about Jen, and the older ones were likely to know the most. . . .

"Hey there, beautiful," an unexpected voice slurred, just inches from her ear. "I've never seen *you* before."

Sydney turned around to find a guy wearing Hawaiian-print trunks and a self-satisfied smile, a plastic lei draped over his bare chest. He tilted a wet plastic cup in her direction, foam sloshing over its rim.

"You look lonely," he announced.

"I'm not," she said coolly, her most recent frat party still fresh in her mind.

"Hard to get, huh," he said before taking a swig of beer. "Girls usually don't like to play that game with me."

He winked in an obvious attempt to convey what a superstud he was. Sydney shook her head, repulsed, and walked away. He whistled at her rear view, making her wish she could march back over and deck him, but a flash of red hair near the edge of the crowd suddenly caught her eye. She joined Roxy with relief.

"I see you've met Maxwell," Roxy said, glancing over Sydney's shoulder. "I could tell you stories about that guy that take *sleaze* to a whole new level. Judging by your reaction, though, you've already figured him out."

Sydney shrugged. "He's not exactly subtle. Anyway, I wanted to thank you again. For everything. *You* know."

She was afraid to mention Francie's name in case anyone overheard.

"Not a problem! I could tell right away you were someone we needed, and it turns out that other girl had a conflict with the Aloha anyway." Roxy rubbed the fingers of her right hand against her thumb, suggesting a money shortage. "Everything worked out fine."

"Still. I owe you."

Roxy grinned happily. "What are sisters for? Besides, it's fun to have some new people around."

Her smile turned suddenly wistful. "Things have been a little sad lately. . . ."

Sydney made herself count to three before she pounced on the opening. "I heard about the girl who died."

Roxy gave her a startled look. "Heard? Ashley said you knew Jen."

"That's right. I did." Her heart raced as she realized her mistake: Of course these girls told each other everything. Maybe she shouldn't have claimed to know Jen after all. "We weren't close, but it was still a shock. And you . . . were you close?"

Roxy nodded. Tears welled into her eyes, reflecting tiki torches. "The closest. Jen was an angel. I just . . . It's hard now, you know? Being in the sorority without her. Pretending to still care . . ."

Roxy wiped her wet eyes with her fingers, spreading streaks of mascara out toward her temples. "I shouldn't be telling you this," she said, sniffing back more tears. "You're new, and all gung-ho. And it really *is* a great group of girls. . . ."

"No, I understand," Sydney assured her, moved by the obvious depth of Roxy's feelings. Somehow it made her feel better, knowing that Jen had had true friends inside the sorority.

"But now I feel stupid." Roxy wiped at her makeup again. "Not to mention scary-looking."

Sydney smiled sympathetically, unable to deny it. "Well . . . it wouldn't hurt if one of us had a tissue."

Roxy nodded toward the fraternity house. "I doubt they have anything as refined as Kleenex in there, but maybe I'll go dunk my face in a sink."

"I'll come with you," Sydney offered.

"No, do me a favor and find Michelle. Did you meet Michelle? Curly brown hair? I think she's wearing yellow tonight. Tell her I said to keep an eye on Katie while I'm gone. She'll know what I mean."

"Okay."

If someone named Katie needed watching, Sydney definitely wanted to find out why.

The music started before she'd taken more than a few steps, the speakers cranked so loud that no one could talk without shouting over the CD. Sydney wove through the crush of people, smiling at the girls she recognized. At last she located Michelle, a slightly sour-looking brunette stationed near the keg.

"Michelle? Hi!" Sydney shouted.

Michelle nodded without smiling. Sydney pointed to the lettering on her pink shirt.

"I'm Sydney Bristow. I don't think we had a chance to talk the other night."

Michelle shrugged.

This is going well, Sydney thought. Just then the song came to an end.

"Roxy sent me to find you," she blurted out in

the break. "She had to go inside, and she wants you to keep an eye on Katie. She said you'd know what that means."

A slight smile straightened the girl's pursed lips. "What's Roxy doing?"

"Just . . . well . . . we were talking about Jen, and it made her kind of sad. She'll be back out pretty soon."

"Oh." Michelle gave Sydney a probing look. "Is she okay?"

"She will be. She just needs a few minutes."

Michelle sighed, her gaze shifting off into the distance. "Nothing's been the same since Jen died. We all just loved her so much. It's . . . not real. We can't believe what happened."

Sydney shifted her weight a few times, wondering how best to exploit this opportunity.

"You don't think . . . Katie?" she offered tentatively.

"She's drunk, but she's not that drunk! I'll cut her off if I have to." Michelle shook her head fiercely. "And if Doug comes anywhere near her . . ."

"Oh." Suddenly Katie's need for being watched seemed a lot less sinister. "Bad relationship?"

"Don't get me started."

The music blared again, to cheers from the growing crowd. Sydney wandered away from Michelle in search of other leads.

In a flat corner of the yard, a group of people had

begun dancing on the grass. Sydney quickly spotted Francie tearing up the makeshift dance floor. She stood and watched for a few seconds before noticing Ashley just feet away, her eyes on the dancers as well.

"Hey, Ashley! How's it going?" Sydney asked, walking to the girl's side.

Ashley gave her a cool sideways glance. "Hello."

"Great party."

"If you like this sort of thing." Ashley shook her head, her salon-perfect hair brushing tanning-bed shoulders. "I don't know why, just once, these guys couldn't get a real band. And something to drink besides beer. Not to mention those tacky lights! You can practically smell the trailer park in here."

Sydney laughed. Ashley hadn't changed her haughty attitude—but this time she had a point.

"That loser Maxwell hit on me earlier," Sydney said confidingly. "What a slime!"

Ashley whipped her head around. "Well, it's not as if *I* like him," she said, fixing Sydney with a piercing look. "Who said I did?"

"Nobody!"

For the second time that night, Sydney realized that all these new people around her weren't new to each other. They had existing, intertwined relationships—ones she didn't understand. She'd have to be more careful of what she said.

"They'd better not." Ashley tossed her blond hair and tilted her chin away, still miffed.

"No one said anything like that. Mostly they've just been saying how much they miss Jen."

"Oh." Not a trace of emotion crossed Ashley's face. She kept her gaze on the dancers.

"I mean, because she was really nice."

"To some people."

Sydney digested that comment, wondering what to make of it. "I guess she could be a little snobby sometimes," she ventured.

"Snobby? No, she—" Ashley cut herself off abruptly. "Jen was fine. I have to go talk to someone."

She stalked off without another word, her back as stiff as her voice had been. Sydney watched her accost a reeling, pixie-haired girl and force her into a conversation.

Could that be Katie? Sydney wondered.

But the possibility didn't seem worth following up on just then. Her head was spinning, from the questions, the crowd, the music, the smoke. . . .

And then there was Maxwell.

"Hey, babe," he said, sidling up to her again. He seemed to have greased his chest since the last time she'd seen him; it was now as oily as his manner. "Bang-Bang Maxwell's here. Tell Daddy what you want."

I want to be sick, Sydney thought. *I want to puke into a plastic bag and break it over your head.*

"You know what I want?" she cooed instead, unable to resist the double payback. "I want you to go be nice to Ashley."

"Ashley!" Maxwell snorted. "Been there, done that. *If* you catch my meaning." He high-fived himself like a total fool. "But *you* . . . you intrigue me."

That's because I could kill you fifteen different ways, she thought, backing away.

"*And* I like your shirt," he added, reaching to touch a rhinestone in a spot where his finger had no business being.

Sydney grabbed his groping hand, stopping it an inch from her body.

"Whoa, you're strong!" he said. She could tell by the way he was squinting that her grip was hurting his fingers.

"Try to remember that next time," she said, squeezing harder. "If I want you to touch me, I'll let you know."

"Do that," he said huskily, turning her threat into an invitation. "Anytime."

She tossed his hand away, disgusted.

"Where are you staying?" he asked. "I could come by later."

"Or not. Listen, I have to go talk to someone." She

bailed before he could catch his breath, pulling off an Ashley-like exit.

I may be sorority material after all, she thought, glancing back to make sure she had lost him.

The gate to the yard stood open a short distance away. Sydney slipped through it into the darker night outside, wanting a quiet moment alone. She had made progress that evening, getting to know more people and how each one felt about Jen. Now she needed to plan her next step.

Everyone liked Jen except Ashley, she remembered, walking the outside perimeter of the fence. Overgrown pine trees bordered her path, turning it into a dark, secluded alley. *Still, that doesn't make Ashley a killer. From what I've seen of her so far, it's entirely possible she's just a—*

A slight noise behind her made Sydney freeze. A hand slapped her posterior, sending her into overdrive.

"That's *it*!" she snapped, wheeling around. A punch flew out from her shoulder before she saw where her fist was going. The only things she knew for sure just then were that she could level a frat boy—and that this one richly deserved it.

But a strong forearm slammed into hers, deflecting her punch. Her hand continued through the air with so much force behind it that she lost her balance and staggered into her opponent.

"Ooh!" said Noah Hicks, chuckling as he

steadied her back to her feet. "Lousy stance. I could have had you right there."

"You *think* you could have," she retorted, annoyed.

"Please. I know I could have."

There was no question he was right. That knowledge, combined with his smug expression, only angered her more.

"What are you doing here?" she demanded. "Spying on me now?"

"Well, you know. Got to keep in practice."

He tried one of his charming smiles, the kind that made him look more boy-next-door than SD-6 superagent, but Sydney wasn't buying. The fact that she'd spent whole days just aching to be alone with him was completely forgotten.

Ever since Paris he's been treating me like I have the plague. And now he sneaks up behind me and smacks my butt? I don't think so.

Noah seemed to read her mind. The smile died suddenly on his lips. He pushed a nervous hand back through his short brown hair.

"You're not happy to see me?" he asked.

"Would that shatter your ego? Did you think I'd trail you around forever, just waiting for you to notice?"

His expression hardened. "Is that what you've been doing?"

"You wish!"

It was on the tip of her tongue to tell him she was seeing someone else now, that Paris had been a fluke. But Paris *hadn't* been a fluke, and standing beside him in darkness again, she was barely two seconds away from throwing herself into his arms.

Something told her he wouldn't fight it. Something told her it was why he had come.

He pointed to her shirt. "You're pledging a sorority now?"

"Wilson didn't tell you?"

"He knows? I'm amazed he'd allow such a waste of time."

Sydney's brows rose. Noah seemed completely unaware of her new mission.

"Besides, you don't seem the type," he added before she could fill him in. "All girly and giggly and stuff."

She might have agreed with him overall, but his choice of words incensed her.

"I'm not girly. Good to know."

"You know what I mean," he said, pained.

"Yes, I think I do."

She turned and headed back the way she had come, Noah right behind her.

"Don't tell me you're mad about *that*!" he said, close on her heels. "That would be very stupid."

"You're right. This whole thing between us is stupid."

"I just wanted to see you. That's all."

"And now you have."

The open gate came into view. Sydney headed straight for it, not slackening her pace a bit. There was no way Noah would follow her into the Triple Chi yard, not with so many people around.

"Sydney!" he called behind her.

She stepped through the gate, back into the party. Back into the noise and music and smoke . . . Back into the normal world, where guys like Noah didn't exist.

Roxy was waiting just inside, her makeup fixed and her features sharp with interest.

"Boyfriend?" she asked, nodding in Noah's direction.

Sydney looked just in time to see him slink into the night. "Hardly," she said, disgusted.

Roxy laughed. "I know what you need."

Tossing an arm across Sydney's shoulders, she led her to the keg.

* * *

Sydney reentered her room from the bathroom to find the lights still blazing and Francie sitting up in bed, a calculator in her hands.

"This is never going to work," she said, frantically punching buttons. "Kira needs the Aloha money tomorrow." She glanced at her alarm clock. "Today," she corrected herself with a moan.

"I thought you were going to put the last few hundred on your credit card." Unwrapping the wet towel from around her head, Sydney looked for a brush.

Francie held up her calculator, pointing to its minuscule screen. "Do you know what that interest comes out to? It'll be all I can do to keep up with the minimum! I'll never be able to pay off the whole amount."

"I told you I'd lend you some money." Settling for a comb, she began forcing it through her wet tangles.

"You can't afford to lend me that kind of money." Francie tossed the calculator onto the floor, a muscle working along her jaw. "I'll have to drop my pledge."

"But you had a great time tonight!"

The first tear made its break, tracing the side of Francie's nose. "I'm just being practical."

"You don't have to be."

Impulsively, Sydney opened her bottom desk drawer, removing a small box way at the back—her emergency fund from Wilson.

"Use it as you see fit, for anything related to your safety, your cover, or your missions," he'd said, giving her the stack of hundreds. "Spies don't always have time for the ATM."

Now Sydney peeled off eight bills and handed them to Francie. "Is this enough?"

Francie blinked a couple of times, then abruptly remembered to breathe, a long, hissing inhalation. "What are you doing keeping that kind of cash in a drawer?"

"I just got it out, in case we needed it for the trip," Sydney lied, closing the box before Francie could see how much money was left. "Just take it and stop worrying. You can pay me back later."

She had expected to make Francie's night, but her friend's eyes narrowed suspiciously. "This is all from your job at the bank?"

"And some birthday money."

"You were broke at the beginning of the year. *Flat* broke," Francie reminded her.

"Yeah, well . . . things change, Francie. I thought you'd be happy, but if you don't want it . . ."

Sydney reached for the money, but Francie snatched it away, her fingers crumpling the crisp bills.

"No, I do. It's just . . . Thanks," she said awkwardly. "I'll find a way to pay you back."

"I know," Sydney said, sighing as she turned off the light.

Wilson would give her a load more cash for Oahu.

And Francie was going to keep track of every penny she spent.

"THIS PLACE IS AMAZING!" Francie exclaimed, gazing around the luxurious, open-air
lobby of the Waikiki Princess hotel.

Sydney nodded, overwhelmed. Forty-five
sorority girls in matching pink Alpha Aloha
T-shirts barely filled one corner of the huge space,
and Sydney didn't know whether to focus on the
clear turquoise ocean a hundred yards out, the
lavishly landscaped swimming pool closer in, or
the enormous tropical flower arrangements
crowning marble pedestals around the lobby. All
the girls were excited, chattering in loud voices,
and even with a handful of room keys to give out,

Roxy was having a hard time getting her sisters' attention.

"All right, all right," she said again, waving one hand over her head. "I know I can't compete with those guys Kira had meet us at the plane. . . ."

Her comment was greeted by cheers as the girls registered their approval of the six bare-chested hunks who had enriched their airport experience with orchid leis and cheek kisses. Kira blushed at the approbation, while Keisha simply smiled, perhaps reliving slipping that twenty into a tapa loincloth.

Ever since their plane had left L.A., some spell had come over the girls. For the first half of the flight they had been pretty quiet—then the energy had started to build. Rubber-band fights had broken out, despite the flight attendants' repeated warnings. Amanda had locked herself into the bathroom to spray pink streaks in her hair, and soon everyone was doing it. And anyone who was twenty-one had her finger on the call button, ordering drink after drink. Since claiming their luggage and sitting through the shuttle ride to the hotel, people had sobered up, but girls still leaned unsteadily into each other, arms thrown fondly around shoulders, waists, and anything else that didn't move out of the way.

"All right!" Roxy broke in determinedly. "The sooner I get these keys passed out, the sooner we can hit the beach!"

More cheering greeted this announcement, stalling her again. When at last the girls settled down, Roxy handed out keys, assigning two girls to each room. She teamed Sydney with Francie, keeping the leftover single for herself.

"I thought we pledges might room with sisters," Sydney objected softly as she took her key. "You know, people who can tell us more about the sorority."

And Jen's death, she added to herself.

But Roxy made a face. "There's plenty of time for all that. Besides, I know you and Francie get along."

Sydney accepted the key without further comment, but when she turned around, the look Francie gave her made her squirm.

"You don't want to room with me?" Francie asked, hurt.

"It's not that," Sydney assured her. "It's just that we already know each other and . . . I thought it would be nice to meet other people."

"Meet whoever you want," Francie sniffed, grabbing her suitcase and dragging it toward an elevator.

"Francie!" Sydney groaned, walking along behind her. "I *want* to room with you. We can meet more people later."

"Really?"

"Of course. A bunch of girls are hitting the beach now. Or we could join those sisters going shopping in Honolulu. Plus there's that luau here tonight. We'll have plenty of opportunities to meet other people."

"No. I meant, do you really want to room with me?"

"That depends. Are you going to wait for me to go back and get my suitcase?"

Francie shrugged, then smiled. "Okay," she relented. "Deal."

* * *

"This really is paradise, isn't it?" Sydney sighed, stirring the pink juice in her coconut with an umbrella-topped swizzle stick. The too-sweet blend of exotic fruits was something she'd never drink at home, but out on the terraced decks of the Waikiki Princess, the molten orange sun just dipping into the Pacific, it seemed exactly right.

"It doesn't suck," Roxy replied with a grin. She was wearing a blue hibiscus-print dress that evening, her bright hair tumbling in perfect waves down her sunburned back. "Even the air feels different here. Did you notice when we got off the plane?"

"Definitely."

Oahu was far more humid than Los Angeles, where even a hint of moisture sent the locals running for air-conditioned cover.

"It's like stepping into a different world," Roxy said, her eyes scanning the scene in front of them.

The Waikiki Princess was new, but its Saturday-night luau already featured prominently in tourist guides everywhere. The chef spared no expense, serving up everything from an array of fresh local seafood to hand-pounded poi on banana leaves. Even now, elaborately decorated tables were being arranged in groups around the swimming pool, and a small stage had been erected beside the man-made waterfall at the deep end. Farther out, near the edge of the sandy beach, a wisp of smoke rose from the traditional underground pig-roasting pit, promising delicious things to come.

"There you are!" Francie called. "We've been looking for you guys."

Francie and Keisha walked up with Gretchen and Emily, two sisters Sydney had met on the beach that afternoon. Like Sydney and Roxy—and everyone else in AKX—the four new arrivals were decked out in their best aloha wear, exuberantly flowered dresses styled to take advantage of the tropical climate. The orchid leis of that morning had also reappeared, reclaimed from the in-room mini refrigerators, where they'd been keeping fresh.

"I can't wait to eat poi!" Gretchen offered. "I've never tried it before."

Keisha's smile spoke of personal experience. "If you're like most people, you'll never try it again."

"I had a bag of taro chips today, and they were good," Francie put in. "Poi's just made of taro."

"Uh-huh. Would you say they were as good as potato chips?" Keisha asked.

Francie looked crestfallen. "Well, no."

"Now imagine soaking them in water and beating them into a gluey purple paste."

Gretchen swallowed hard. "The *pig's* going to be good," she ventured.

"The pig's going to be very good," Roxy reassured her. "And who knows? You might like the poi, too."

"Maybe with catsup?" Emily suggested.

Sydney smiled to herself as she followed her new sisters down to the pool terrace. Maybe it was jet lag from the time difference, or the lingering effects of too much afternoon sun, but Sydney couldn't remember the last time she'd felt so relaxed—or so included. Being in a sorority wasn't awful at all. It was actually pretty cool.

With the sun below the horizon, the sky slowly darkened to purple. Brass tiki torches bloomed in blue and orange flames against the dark green vegetation. Everything seemed softer than in California: the flower-scented air, the trade winds rustling the densely packed palms. Faces glowed in the torchlight, shapes blurring and running together as people moved through the darkness.

Suddenly the stage came to life. A gentle spotlight, more like a moonbeam, lit its center as a drum began to beat, the ancient rhythm raising goose bumps on Sydney's bare arms. Male dancers ran out, their heads and ankles encircled by thick wreaths of green ferns. The large, milling crowd of hotel guests began to move, wandering to the grass in front of the stage.

"This is so cool," Francie whispered, taking a place beside Sydney.

Sydney grinned happily. "It is. I'm glad we're here together."

The girls linked arms, swaying to the beat. The men were soon joined by female dancers, who put on quite a show before a man in a suit bounded onto the stage, a microphone in his hand.

"Alooooooooooh-ha!" he greeted the crowd.

"Alooooooooooh-ha!" they echoed loudly, full of island spirit.

"Ladies and gentlemen, *wahines* and *kanes*, welcome to our luau. Dinner is served!"

The drumming resumed as four men in native dress trotted into the dining area, a beautifully roasted pig on a leaf-covered litter between them. The crowd applauded appreciatively, then began filling chairs at the waiting tables. Sydney and Francie found a table with a few sisters they knew and a few more they didn't, and when Roxy joined them as well, Sydney felt a rush of genuine pleasure.

The food was served in course upon course, traditional Hawaiian dishes, such as roast pork, sweet potatoes, poi, and leaf-wrapped bundles of fish, mixed with mainland favorites like chewy sourdough rolls, grilled shrimp, and crème brûlée. Sydney tried not to overeat, in case she needed to be on her toes later, but everything was so delicious. By the time the meal was over, she thought she knew how muumuus had gotten so popular.

"I'm stuffed!" she groaned, pushing back from the table. "And the scary thing is, that chocolate mousse is still calling my name."

"I hope you're not too full to dance," Roxy said with a mischievous smile. "Because someone might have signed us up for hula lessons after this."

"Who would do such a heinous thing?" Keisha demanded. "Oh, wait. Let me guess."

"It was *me*!" Roxy cried, as if revealing a big secret. "They're going to teach us over at the stage."

"Oh, joy."

Keisha rolled her eyes, but Sydney already saw through her fake jadedness. None of the Alphas wanted to seem young, or inexperienced, or—worst of all—eager. Keisha's solution was to pretend everything either bored or disgusted her before she went ahead and did it anyway. She was actually pretty amusing, once a person figured her out.

I wonder if I'd have caught on so fast if it weren't for SD-6, Sydney mused. She had always been a good judge of character, but the techniques she'd learned from the CIA had moved her light-years ahead in sizing up new people.

The waiters came around and began clearing dishes.

"When does all this dancing take place?" Francie asked.

"Any second now," Roxy replied.

Rising from her chair, she began circulating among the tables, telling the sisters to go wait in front of the stage. Judging from their reactions, Sydney wasn't the only one who hadn't expected to hula when the dessert tray was going around, but soon all the Alphas were gathered on the designated patch of grass, awaiting Roxy's orders.

Their president joined them shortly, with Kira and three female dancers in tow. The dancers took the stage, directing the girls to spread out on the grass and form rows. Sydney ended up in front, surrounded by Roxy, Kira, Alyssa, and Val. Soft slack-key guitar music floated out of hidden speakers, and the hula lesson got under way.

"When we do the hula, we are not just dancing. We are telling a story with our bodies and our movements," the lead dancer explained. "The hula is a very ancient tradition, and should be performed with respect."

"Somebody should have told me that before my second mai tai," Katie quipped from a few rows back, but the resulting giggles were quickly squelched.

The dancers demonstrated basic steps, and soon Sydney had kicked off her sandals, her bare feet moving over the grass in an easy, relaxed rhythm. She was really starting to feel it when Roxy leaned over to whisper.

"There goes Ashley," she said, hiking a thumb back over her shoulder. "Off on another of her disappearing acts."

Sydney turned in time to see Ashley drift away from one end of the back row and blend into the darkness of the outer hotel grounds.

"Disappearing act? She probably has to use the restroom or something."

Roxy shook her head. "She does this all the time. Takes off on her own, like she's too good for us, with no explanations, ever."

"Takes off to do what?"

Roxy shrugged and resumed dancing. "Who knows? She tries to be so sly about it. I honestly think she believes I don't notice, but really I just don't care."

Sydney glanced behind her again. Ashley was

nowhere to be seen. And suddenly all Sydney's senses were screaming a red alert.

"Oh!" she groaned, pressing both hands against her abdomen. "I wouldn't mind finding a bathroom. I shouldn't have eaten so much."

"Are you okay?" Roxy asked, concerned.

"Yeah, I'll be back."

"I hope you feel better," Roxy called after her.

Sydney could hear Francie asking questions behind her as she beelined for the lobby. She hoped her friend wouldn't try to follow her to the bathroom, since she had no intention of actually going there. Reaching the upper terrace, she hurried into the hotel lobby on the ocean side, strode quickly across its plush carpeting, and emerged into the front parking loop off the street. If Ashley *was* planning to pull a disappearing act, she didn't have much of a head start—and Sydney planned to find out where she was going.

Sure enough, she had barely stepped onto the pavement when Ashley materialized out of the landscaping along the right side of the hotel. She had put on a navy blue hat, her blond hair tucked tightly inside it. A long, dark windbreaker had also appeared out of nowhere, covering her Hawaiian-print dress. Sydney's heart slammed into her rib cage—hiding clothing in hotel bushes definitely qualified as suspicious behavior. Ducking quickly behind a column, determined to learn what the girl was up to, she watched as Ashley crossed the street and headed north. A bus rumbled up and stopped at the curb, temporarily blocking Sydney's view. When it rolled off again, Ashley was gone.

In the bus! Sydney realized, sprinting after it.

She had run only a block when a taxi stopped at the corner to let out two elderly tourists.

"Are you free? Can I ride?" Sydney yelled at the driver, grabbing the open cab door. "I'm kind of in a hurry."

"Where are you going?" he asked suspiciously.

"I . . . don't know," she admitted.

He tried to drive away, but she held on to the door.

"My girlfriend just got into a bus, and I was supposed to meet her, but I was late, and it went that way." She lied as fast as she could, pointing up the street. "She didn't tell me where we're going, but I really have to catch her. I'll pay you double," she added, borrowing a trick she'd learned from Noah.

As in Paris, the offer worked like magic.

The cabbie shrugged. "Hop in."

By the time he pulled into traffic again, the bus had been lost in the distance. But it had to stop for passengers and the taxi didn't, and soon Sydney's car was just off its bumper. They had trailed it about three miles, Sydney praying the entire way that Ashley hadn't already exited somewhere, when the bus door opened again and a girl in a dark hat and windbreaker climbed out.

"Yes!" Sydney breathed, relieved. "That's my friend," she told the cabbie. "You can let me out here."

He raised an eyebrow. "Here?"

"Yes, here," she said impatiently, fishing a twenty out of her bra. "What's wrong with here?"

"Well . . . it's nighttime, this is Chinatown, and if you'll excuse me for saying so, your outfit is *screaming* tourist."

"I can take care of myself," she assured him, handing over the money and stepping out onto the sidewalk.

He hesitated. For a moment she was afraid he wouldn't leave her. Then he shrugged and drove away.

Up ahead, Ashley turned a corner, heading inland. She seemed completely unaware of Sydney's presence as she walked briskly down the street. Sydney kept to the shadows, hanging back far enough to remain undetected. But when Ashley turned onto Hotel Street, Sydney knew something big was up. Even cursory research produced numerous mentions of crime and prostitution on that notorious street. And while it had supposedly been cleaned up in recent years, it still looked seamy to Sydney. It was inconceivable that Ashley could have personal business there.

Unless she wants a tattoo, Sydney thought,

scuttling quickly past the windows of a brightly lit parlor.

Moments later Ashley turned again, taking a dark side street to a run-down metal warehouse. Sydney watched as she fished a slip of paper from her pocket, compared it to the street numbers over the door, then let herself into the unlocked building.

Sloppy, thought Sydney, creeping closer. *I'd have memorized that address.*

Deeming it too risky to enter through the door Ashley had used, Sydney stole along the side of the darkened building, looking for a window. The wall at street level was solid tin, but eight feet up, a row of windows beckoned. Sydney spotted an open one, then wasted precious seconds searching for something to stand on. By the time she'd found a metal trash can, overturned it, and climbed silently onto that shaky platform, Ashley was deep in conversation with two strange men around a puddle of candlelight near the center of the big, empty building.

This is no good, Sydney thought nervously.

She was taking a big chance by spying where someone might see her, and she was still too far away to hear a single word. She couldn't even see faces with the lousy angle she had. Ashley's dark hat covered hers, and both of her male contacts had cinched the hoods of their sweatshirts until only their eyes peeked out. Sydney suspected that the bulges in their waistbands were guns; she knew for sure that Ashley's buddies weren't frat boys. In fact, they were exactly the sort of characters she would have expected stuck-up Ashley to run from, shrieking in terror.

Unless she knows them. Unless they're under-cover agents!

Sydney watched, her mind sorting through the possibilities, until one of the men shook Ashley's hand, indicating the meeting was over. Sydney climbed down abruptly, her risk of exposure becoming too great. Two minutes later, spying from a doorway across the street, she saw the men slink out the front of the warehouse.

There was no sign of Ashley.

Should I go in there? she wondered, shifting anxiously in her hiding place.

Is there a back exit?

Did they kill her?

She was still trying to decide on a plan when Ashley appeared in the doorway, unharmed. In fact, she seemed to be smiling, her teeth flashing white in the darkness. She looked carefully up and down the street, then pulled off her hat and shook out her hair, no longer worried about being seen.

So, that's it, then, Sydney thought, stunned. *I've found my sister spy.*

5

EARLY THE NEXT MORNING, Sydney stood among the mangroves in a deserted cove deep at the inland edge of Pearl Harbor, totally absorbed with planning that night's mission.

It hadn't been hard sneaking out of the hotel, leaving everyone else sleeping in. After the luau the night before, most of the girls had gone on to look for more fun, and by the time Sydney had returned from Chinatown, everyone had scattered. No one had even seemed to realize she'd been missing.

No one except Francie, who had been half frantic thinking Sydney was sick, or lost, or both. Sydney had had to make up a lie about using the bathroom in the hotel lounge—closer than their sixteenth-floor room—then lying down on the ladies' room sofa and unexpectedly nodding off. Since she had only been gone for ninety minutes, Francie had bought it, although not very happily.

"I didn't know *what* happened to you," she'd complained. "You could have been attacked by bears."

"In Hawaii?" Sydney had replied skeptically.

"Sharks, then. I don't know. Are you avoiding me?"

"Of course not!"

"Because ever since we started hanging out with these girls, you've been acting really weird."

"What are you talking about?"

"Like you'd rather be with them than with me. Like you're changing your whole personality!"

"Francie, I got a little food poisoning or something. That's all."

She had smoothed things over by promising to go sightseeing the next day, but instead, she had risen at dawn, pulled on some running clothes, and slipped out of their room.

Hopefully Francie's still sleeping, she thought now, taking out a pair of miniature, nonreflective binoculars. If she got back at a reasonable hour, looking sweaty enough, Francie would assume she'd been jogging. It would never occur to her that she'd

...tually picked up a rental car, switched on her GPS unit, and taken a ten-mile drive up the coast.

Sydney trained her lenses out over the enormous three-lobed harbor. She couldn't begin to see all of it from where she stood. She couldn't even see her dive site with certainty, just an expanse of wind-whipped water a long way out from shore. Her goal that morning was simply to get a feel for what she'd be up against later, when she would dive in total darkness.

Far off in the distance, navy ships floated at their moorings on Ford Island, the large landmass near the center of the harbor where the battleship *Arizona* had been resting when the Japanese attacked. For a moment, Sydney envisioned the panic of that day superimposed over the calm of the present. Smoke billowed from bombed and torpedoed ships, strafing aircraft screamed low overhead, hundreds of terrified young Americans did their best to rally, fighting for their lives. . . .

She dropped her binoculars, more resolved than ever to find Dr. Suler's prototype. The world had changed since 1941, but war was just as ugly. She would do anything in her power to prevent another Pearl Harbor. Anything at all.

The water here is so murky, she thought, staring into the shallows next to shore. Unlike the crystalline open ocean, the water in the harbor was a dark, soupy green. *No wonder nobody knows what's down there—visibility's going to stink. And that's a long swim out.*

Even so, starting from this overgrown backwater fifty yards off a public roadway was safer than infiltrating a base, where she'd be a hundred times more likely to arouse suspicion. A boat was still out of the question, though—too likely to be spotted.

I'll get an underwater scooter, she decided. She had practiced with the propeller-driven devices as part of her SD-6 scuba training. On land, a scooter was heavy, but once in the water, it would save both her energy and her oxygen by towing her to the dive site. She would travel underwater, so no one could track her from shore, and when she arrived she would have all her strength left for the dive.

Her decision made, Sydney hurried back up the gentle slope to her rental car. The place she had chosen to park, a packed-dirt turnout on the harbor side of the road, wasn't invisible, but the surrounding vegetation provided a good screen. At night, her black compact car would be impossible to spot.

Okay, here's what I need, she thought, making a mental list as she steered back onto the pavement and headed toward the nearest dive shop. *The scooter, mask, fins, tank, dive light, dive bag . . . Should I get a knife?*

It couldn't hurt, in case she encountered something she needed to cut. Or pry. Or kill.

Like a shark.

She shuddered at the idea. At night, in such murky water, a shark would be on top of her before she even saw it. Not that she'd be able to outswim it if she did . . .

Maybe sharks don't like the harbor, she comforted herself. *They're probably all out in the ocean, harassing the fish.*

Wait. I think they eat seals.

She shuddered again, the fine hairs rising on the back of her neck. The black wet suit she'd be wearing would give her a definite seal-like quality. . . .

I've got nukes, spies, and an angry roommate. I refuse to think about sharks!

* * *

"Where have you been?" Francie demanded the second Sydney stepped into their room. She was sitting on her unmade bed wearing a pink miniskirt and halter top, a straw hat tilted back on her head. "We're going to be late to breakfast!"

"No, we aren't," Sydney promised, pulling the door closed behind her. "I'll just rinse off, put on some clean shorts, and be ready. Five minutes, tops."

"Half the girls are already down there," Francie complained. "We have that poolside buffet this morning, remember?"

"Then go down without me. I'll catch up."

Rushing to her suitcase, Sydney pulled out a fresh tank top. The "sweat" on the one she was wearing had come straight from a bottle of Evian, but Francie didn't know that.

"I don't *want* to go without you," Francie said. "I've been doing everything without you."

"That's not true."

"It feels that way. You've been bouncing all over the place ever since we got here."

Sydney grabbed the rest of the clothes she needed. "Maybe. A little. But there are all these other girls, and so many things to do. Aren't you having fun?"

"I guess. It's just . . . We're still going sightseeing after breakfast, right? Just you and me?"

"And the sooner I get in the shower, the sooner we can leave."

Francie gestured for her to hurry, and Sydney ran into the bathroom. Standing under a flood of hot water, soaping as fast as she could, she tried to figure out what was going on with her best friend.

Francie hasn't been herself since I mentioned *AKX.*

All the complaints—about snootiness, about money, about Sydney's activities—none of that was like Francie at all. And if Sydney had been a bit more outgoing than usual, Francie had been twice as clingy.

It's almost like . . . She's jealous! Sydney realized.

Aside from her buddy Todd on the track team, Sydney hadn't made any other close friends at school. She and Francie were best friends, roommates, confidants. In fact, they'd been pretty much joined at the hip ever since they'd met during the summer.

"I'm almost ready!" Sydney called out, filled with sudden understanding.

"Yeah, sure," Francie called back grumpily. "You're going downstairs with wet hair?"

"Yes," Sydney answered immediately. "If it makes you happy, you bet I am!"

* * *

Sydney's was the only wet head at the sorority's private poolside buffet. Her white tank and denim shorts comprised the least dressy outfit, and she was the only girl there whose face was completely free of makeup. While she hadn't felt self-conscious leaving her room that way, she was starting to think that she'd made a mistake.

"Maybe I *should* have dried my hair," she whispered to Francie as they grabbed plates and joined the line for food. "Geez. I thought people would be down here in their bathing suits."

Francie shook her head disbelievingly. "Are you kidding? Have you been paying attention at all?"

"To what?"

"The uniforms!" Francie whispered. "These girls have a uniform for everything—they just don't tell us what it is."

"That's crazy!" said Sydney, making a face. Then she looked around her. With the exception of her and Roxy—who always went her own way— every sister there was wearing a short skirt and wide-brimmed sun hat.

"Who tipped *you* off?" she asked Francie.

"I'm getting the hang of it now, that's all."

Sydney gave her a skeptical look.

Francie smiled sheepishly, caught. "And I might have overheard some girls talking last night."

"Thanks for the heads-up."

The line moved forward and Sydney started filling her plate. Bypassing the scrambled eggs, bacon, and pastries, she loaded up on fresh tropical fruit.

"I'll get us a table," she told Francie.

Grabbing a fork, she turned around and nearly walked right into Ashley.

Miss Perfect was wearing another of her immaculate all-pink ensembles. Her lip curled disapprovingly as she looked Sydney up and down.

"Late night?" she asked sarcastically. Her snobby tone was so L.A., it was almost *too* L.A. Sydney had noticed that before, but now she suddenly wondered if Ashley might be covering another accent—a foreign accent.

"I could ask you the same thing," she replied.

Ashley blanched. "What's that supposed to mean?"

"Just that I saw you leave the hula lesson. And I didn't see you after. Hot date?"

"None of your business!" snapped Ashley. Spinning on the heel of one designer sandal, she stalked off past the pool and sat at the farthest table.

"Whew!" said Francie. "I think you made her mad."

"Yeah," Katie piped in behind them. "Overreact much?"

Sydney shrugged slightly, her gaze fixed on her new foe. "I'm getting the impression that's how Ashley gets through life."

Katie laughed, delighted. "Gee, you catch on fast!"

"Sydney!" Francie scolded nervously. "It won't help us get initiated if you start a war with Ashley."

"What did I do?" Sydney protested, feigning innocence. "I just asked a simple question."

Not that she'd expected an answer. Still, it couldn't hurt to shake Ashley's tree a little. A properly worded innuendo might even goad her into making a mistake.

"Don't worry about it," said Katie. "Ashley can moan all she wants to, but if Roxy likes you, you're in."

*   *   *

They had just returned from sightseeing and Francie was still in the shower when Sydney's untraceable SD-6 cell phone rang. Lunging for her suitcase, she dug it out from under her clothes and pressed the Talk button.

"Hello?" she whispered, hoping the running water would keep Francie from hearing.

"Hey," said a male voice on the other end. "It's me. Noah."

"Noah?"

She sat down hard, absolutely stunned.

"Listen," he said. "I don't know what happened the other night, but it's all I've been thinking about."

"I just . . . you didn't . . ." She was so surprised by the sound of his voice that she could barely remember either. "You made me mad."

"Yeah. I got that part."

"Oh." Maybe she *had* been a little touchy.

"You could have told me it was a mission," he added. "That would have pretty much cleared things up."

"I know." She sighed. "It's just . . . a lot of things."

"I know."

"Do you?" she asked, wondering if he might actually be admitting something.

"Hey, I just found out you're in Hawaii," he said, switching subjects. "I'm totally jealous!"

"It *is* pretty nice. Francie and I just took the bus to Diamond Head, then went swimming at this beautiful place called Hanauma Bay. The fish are protected there—practically tame."

"How come *you* get all the cushy assignments?" he asked.

"Right. The sewers of Paris. That was *real* cushy."

"What sewer? That was a tunnel."

"Call it whatever you want. It's just a desperate attempt to forget all that stuff floating in the water."

Noah laughed, and so did she. It felt good to talk openly about her job. The shower was still running full blast, and Noah was the only other person in the world who knew—really knew—this secret side of her.

"So where does this fancy sorority of yours bunk up?" he asked. "The Royal Hawaiian?"

"We're in a new place. Waikiki Princess."

"I've heard of it. I've heard it's nice."

"You mean I'm actually someplace you haven't already been?"

"The thing is," Noah teased, laughing, "I've never joined a sorority."

"I miss you," Sydney blurted out, immediately wincing at her own stupidity. That was the *last* thing she should have admitted!

But Noah amazed her again.

"I miss you too," he said.

6

"WHAT'S THIS MEETING ABOUT?" Francie asked as she and Sydney rode the hotel elevator down to the floor below the lobby.

"I don't know," Sydney replied. "Roxy just said to meet in the Aloha Room at four o'clock."

Francie checked her watch. "She didn't give us much warning."

"You know Roxy. Not big on ceremony."

In fact, Sydney had barely hung up with Noah before their room phone had rung and Roxy had informed her of the previously unscheduled event. Francie had had to rush to get her hair dried, and neither of them had any idea what the proper AKX uniform for a surprise meeting was. They had finally decided to go with flowered dresses and crossed fingers.

The elevator doors opened on the Blue Pacific floor. A brass sign indicated that the Aloha Room was to their left.

"Maybe we're going to play more games," Francie suggested as they walked.

"Maybe."

Sydney hoped not. They had played games after breakfast that morning, cutesy bare-your-soul stuff, exactly as Wilson had promised. Luckily for Sydney, the deep and meaningful mysteries her new sisters had wanted to explore had included highly guarded secrets like her favorite type of cookie—chocolate chip—and the name of the first boy she'd ever kissed—Brian Peters, in fourth grade. A game of no-holds-barred Truth or Dare would have been a lot more interesting. Truth was out of the question, but she could have kicked butt on the dares.

"I think Emily cheated to win that crown," Francie said in a low voice.

"I think so too. But since it's made of suckers, let's let her have it."

The friends exchanged smiles, back on the same wavelength, but Sydney's heart was somewhere else. Ever since they'd said good-bye, she'd been yearning for Noah.

It's so like him to be nice when there's nothing I

can do about it, she thought unhappily. *Why can't he be nice in person?*

Still, he'd finally come dangerously close to admitting his feelings for her. That had to be progress.

Inside the Aloha Room, most of the girls had already taken seats. Roxy stood up front, shifting impatiently from foot to foot. She looked ready to burst with good news, and the moment Sydney laid eyes on her, she felt her spirits rise.

"Okay, who's still not here?" Roxy demanded of Kira, who jumped up with a list in her hands. Kira read four names, one of them Ashley's.

"What time is it?" Roxy asked her.

"Five minutes after four."

"Okay. They're late and I'm not waiting anymore." Roxy looked hopefully to the sisters already in seats, inviting them to agree with her.

"Yeah, get it over with," Keisha said. "In case you haven't noticed, it's a lot nicer outside than down here in the basement."

"All right, then. Here it is," Roxy said, her blue eyes round with excitement. "I booked us all on a cruise!"

Pandemonium greeted this unexpected announcement, everyone exclaiming and shouting out questions at once.

"Where are we going?" several voices called in unison.

"Not that type of cruise," Roxy said, laughing. "A catamaran dinner cruise tonight! We're really lucky, because there are so many of us, and it was such short notice. But I got forty-five places on a boat that carries two hundred. We'll have dinner out on the ocean, with a bar and dancing. It's going to be so much fun!"

The girls began talking excitedly, most of them in agreement that a catamaran ride was a big improvement over the original evening schedule, which had them eating on their own with free time afterward.

"One more thing," said Roxy, happy to see her plan so well received. "We used Kira's credit card to reserve all those spaces, so everyone owes her another hundred and fifty. How do you want them to pay you, Kira?"

"Check, I guess. I could take cash from a few people, but if everyone wants to pay that way it'll be too much money to carry around."

"I'll let you guys work that out with Kira," said Roxy. "In the meantime, the hotel shuttle is taking us to the dock at five forty-five and the boat is leaving at six-fifteen. Everyone needs to be ready and in the lobby by five-forty at the *latest*. Any questions?"

No one raised a hand.

"Okay, then. Meeting dismissed!"

Everyone jumped up, eager to pump Roxy for

more details or hand their money over to Kira. Sydney and Francie exchanged less thrilled looks and drifted into the hall.

"*More* money," Francie griped. "At least when we were eating on our own I had the *option* of skipping dinner."

"It is adding up," Sydney admitted.

But she had a much bigger problem. As soon as it got fully dark, she had planned to slip away to carry out her mission in Pearl Harbor. Now she'd be stuck on a boat somewhere—and she didn't even know for how long.

"The thing about this sorority," Francie said glumly, reading her mind, "is that our lives aren't our own anymore. I feel like I'm scrambling all the time just trying to keep up. With the money, the clothes, the schedule, the girls . . ."

"We're new. It'll get easier."

"Hope so," Francie grumbled.

* * *

"This is pretty nice after all," Sydney said, her elbows planted beside Francie's on a side railing. In front of them, the Pacific stretched out to meet another spectacular sunset, and beneath their feet, the hi-tech catamaran rocked just enough to let them know they were on a boat.

"All I can say is, they'd better serve dinner soon," Francie replied, glancing back over her shoulder.

Sydney followed her gaze to the aft-deck bar, where many of the sisters were already working on their second or third pineapple-garnished drinks. Once the men on board had discovered a sorority in their midst, the mai tais and blue Hawaiis had begun flowing freely, in both senses of the word.

"Those blue ones just look . . . wrong," Francie added. "Like drinking Ty-D-Bol."

"Go tell Ashley. She'll be thrilled," Sydney suggested, imagining her reaction to having her cocktail compared to toilet cleaner. Ashley had knocked back more of the blue drinks than anyone; Sydney knew, because she'd been keeping an eye on her rival spy ever since they'd boarded the boat. She didn't expect any forays from Ashley that night—the girl was as trapped as she was—but it never hurt to pay attention.

Strings of tiny white lights had begun to twinkle around the bar and in some of the potted palms ringing the dance floor before dinner was finally announced. The passengers moved into a low-ceilinged salon with a buffet set up along one side and three very long, narrow tables for dining. Roxy made no attempt to separate the sisters from the rest of the guests; everybody helped herself to a plate of food and grabbed the most convenient seat. Conversations and laughter echoed off the walls in the tightly enclosed space, making people talk even louder. Waiters bustled back and forth, keeping the drinks flowing—a task they carried off admirably, considering the demand. Sitting beside Francie, Sydney spotted Ashley near the end of the next table, flirting drunkenly with a man at least fifteen years her senior. She had just decided that the room was becoming uncomfortably hot when a burst of dance music sounded on deck, yanking people up out of their seats.

A passing guy stopped to smile at Francie. "Want to dance?"

"How did you know?" she asked happily, jumping up before remembering Sydney. "Oh. You don't mind if—"

"Go!" Sydney told her. "Have fun."

She barely noticed her friend leaving, her attention was so fixed on Ashley. Did she know that older man? Was it possible he was a contact?

Maybe she's not even drunk!

Sydney could fake intoxication too, although all those drinks Ashley had downed had to be going somewhere.

Maybe she's ordering virgins. The possibility gave her a sick little jab at the pit of her stomach. It made sense; no sane spy would get that impaired in public. But why would Ashley pretend? What was she trying to cover?

Ashley's dinner partner rose abruptly, passing

within twenty feet of Sydney as he left the room. His khakis and Hawaiian shirt couldn't quite erase the businessman from his demeanor, and threads of silver glinted in his dark hair.

He reminded her of Wilson.

That's it! she thought excitedly. *Ashley was drinking because she needed an excuse to hang out with a completely inappropriate man.*

Convinced he was a contact, Sydney rose to her feet and trailed him.

The first place he led her was the men's room, where he disappeared behind a closed door. Unable to risk following him inside, Sydney joined the long line for the ladies', hoping he would emerge again before her turn. He did, heading for the bow of the boat. Sydney followed.

Full darkness had fallen on deck now. The rising moon cast a silver glow over the ocean, but the boat was full of shadows. Sydney moved cautiously, hanging back. The driving music from the aft-deck dance floor covered the sound of her footsteps, the occasional laugh or shout carrying clearly on the warm night air. A long section of rail up ahead was deserted. The man stopped there and looked out to sea a moment, then began digging through his pockets. Sydney tensed.

A flame flickered to life and transferred itself to the end of a cigarette. The man leaned casually against the railing, filling the empty night around him with smoke rings.

Sydney hesitated, confused. Had he really come out there to smoke, or had he sensed her presence? Perhaps he was only stalling, waiting for her to make a move.

She was still trying to decide whether to stay with him or return to shadowing Ashley when a panicked scream from the aft deck jerked her bolt upright. The sound sliced through the loud dance music, horrifying in its intensity. And then the music stopped.

Forgetting about the mysterious man, Sydney turned and ran.

Out on the dance floor, chaos ruled. Everyone was talking and shouting, trying to figure out what had happened. At the center of the biggest knot, only feet from the low side railing, Sydney spotted Ashley, babbling frantically to Roxy and two crewmen. People clustered around them, trying to overhear.

Her sense of foreboding growing, Sydney pushed her way through the crowd.

"That girl! You know, that *girl*!" Ashley kept repeating. "She was right here. I just saw her!"

"Who, Ashley?" Roxy looked scared. "Calm down and tell us what happened."

"It was a splash! You heard it, right, Roxy? You heard the splash?"

"A splash?" one of the crewmen said apprehensively. "What kind of splash?"

Ashley clawed desperately at Roxy's arm. Her glassy eyes rolled Sydney's way and Sydney's insides froze.

She was no longer certain Ashley was faking anything.

"Her!" Ashley screamed, pointing at Sydney. "It was *her* friend."

"Francie? What about Francie?"

Ashley turned away, peering past a fake potted palm and over the edge of the boat. "There was a splash," she repeated, bewildered. "She was dancing right here. And then . . ."

Sydney's knees buckled.

"Man overboard!" both crewmen shouted at the same time. The words electrified the crowd, who picked up the phase and began shouting too.

"Man overboard! Man overboard!"

The crewmen ran off in different directions. Sydney staggered to the nearest railing and looked down ten feet to the ocean, barely able to breathe. *They practice for this. They have drills,* she told herself, struggling to fill her lungs. *Help is on the way. Francie knows how to swim.*

Without making a conscious decision, Sydney climbed up onto the railing, centering her feet beneath her. She crouched a moment, finding her balance, then managed a standing position. The water looked even farther down now, and the moonlight had lost its brilliance. She couldn't see Francie anywhere.

What if Ashley pushed her?

If so, she could have done it a mile back, only now sounding the alarm. The thought made Sydney teeter.

"Hey, you! What are you doing?" someone shouted. "Get down!"

Sydney heard footsteps running toward her. Holding her breath, she jumped.

"Man overboard!"

The cry went up again as she plummeted feet-first into the water, her arms curled over her head for safety the way she had been trained. Her dress billowed over her face, pushed up by water much colder than she'd expected. She kicked upward, breaking the surface only a couple of feet from where she had landed. The boat was already past her and receding at a surprising rate, moving far more quickly than she'd realized while aboard.

"Francie!" she called, turning her back to the catamaran and swimming along its wake. "Francie, can you hear me?"

A swell hit her in the face, filling her open mouth with salt water. She spit and sputtered as the salt burned her nose and throat. Kicking hard to lift her torso above water, she looked all around for any sign of her friend.

"Francie!" she called again.

The ocean was rougher than it had appeared from above. Every swell that lifted her let her see only the moonlit crests of other swells. In the troughs she saw only darkness.

"Francie!"

No answer. No sound at all, except for her own splashing and the distant hum of the cruising ship's motor. She imagined Francie lost somewhere, cold and terrified, and started swimming again. Stroke, stroke, stroke . . . She'd put her strength into covering distance before she tried shouting again.

Suddenly, the beam of a searchlight exploded around her, so bright she was nearly blinded. The captain had turned the boat around and was coming back for the rescue. She heard a collective shout go up at the sight of her.

"Attention, you in the water! We are throwing out a life sling," a voice blared over a bullhorn. "Place the sling around your body and we'll pull you up to safety."

Not likely, Sydney thought, lowering her head and swimming faster. *Not without Francie.*

She could feel herself getting tired. In the back of her mind, she knew her search was probably futile. But if Francie died it would be her fault. Ashley had to have pushed Francie as a way of getting to Sydney. So if anything happened to Francie . . .

"Attention, Sydney!" Francie's voice came over the bullhorn. "Are you completely freaking nuts? Get in that sling *right now*!"

"Francie?" Sydney turned to face the boat, squinting into its spotlight. "Francie," she shouted, "is that you?"

"Of course it's me! Will you get on the boat?"

Sydney stroked to the life sling, totally confused. The crew used a winch to haul her up, her soaked dress clinging in a way that might have been more embarrassing had she been less upset. Her eyes searched out Francie in the crowd, and the moment her feet touched deck she ran to her friend to make sure she was safe.

"What were you thinking?" Francie demanded, wrapping a silver emergency blanket around Sydney's shoulders. "You scared me half to death!"

"I thought you were in the water," said Sydney, still trying to understand. "Ashley said—"

"I was using the bathroom! I do that sometimes," Francie interrupted. "If you would have let these guys do their job, instead of diving off the side like Miss Superhero while—"

"I jumped."

"What?"

"I didn't dive. I jumped," Sydney corrected her meekly.

"Oh, right," Francie said sarcastically. "Hardly dangerous at all then. My mistake."

A crew member touched Sydney's back, interrupting the conversation. "Are you all right?" he asked. He was barely Sydney's age, and his face showed how scared he had been.

"I'm fine," she assured him. "I'm sorry about all the trouble."

"You'll still need to see the onboard medic. And help us fill out an incident report. If you don't mind coming with me . . ."

She followed him through a crowd that parted like the Red Sea, two hundred curious pairs of eyes staring openly into hers. Sydney winced. Not only had her rescue attempt been totally pointless, she had broken the cardinal rule of spying—she had called attention to herself.

"Listen," she said suddenly, grabbing the crewman's elbow. "Ashley said she heard a splash. Was she hallucinating? Did she just make that up?"

The guy gave her a slight, sympathetic smile. "It was probably a big fish jumping. There are plenty of them out there. Your friend had too much to drink and she got confused, that's all."

"Right."

But she didn't believe that for a second. Ashley had portrayed the bumbler so cleverly that Sydney had let her guard down. Until that moment she'd been certain that her own cover was secure, that Ashley couldn't suspect her of being a rival spy. Now she knew how cunning the other girl really was.

She must have planned the whole thing to get me to jump overboard—and maybe be lost at sea in the process. If she suspects I've taken Jen's place, then she knows I'm here on a mission. Has she figured out what it is?

Sydney shivered under her blanket.

It has to be tonight, then. No sane person would expect me to go scuba diving after that fun little swim.

To: Aw23i5pl300
From: SisterAct
Subject: Developing situation

I was right—one of our new pledges
is definitely on the job. All signs
of advanced training verified.
Request permission to make this go
away.

7

THE CLOCK HAD PASSED midnight when Sydney finally slipped away, keeping to the shadows. Nobody knew she was sneaking out, and if all went well, no one ever would.

Francie has to be asleep by now, she thought, skirting a streetlight.

Pleading a headache, Francie had gone up to bed as soon as they'd returned to the hotel. Sydney had entered their room only long enough to change into dry clothes and grab the backpack in which she'd secreted her GPS unit, SD-6 cell phone, and a tightly rolled towel, saying she was going to hang out downstairs. Francie hadn't even looked at her as she left, still upset about what she now referred to as Sydney's stupidity on the boat.

What does Francie think? Sydney wondered, wishing Roxy had never booked them aboard that cruise in the first place. *That I was out there enjoying myself with the sharks?*

She groaned as she slipped around the final corner into the off-site public parking garage where she had parked her rental car. The entire time she'd been in the water trying to rescue Francie, sharks had never once entered her mind. Now, driving out of the garage onto the deserted downtown streets, she knew she'd be unable to forget them. She tried to concentrate on her mission, the prototype, what to do about Ashley . . . but teeth consumed her inner vision. Big, triangular, gnashing teeth, their edges so sharp they could amputate limbs without pain, only the sick, terrifying sensation of an unexpected tug.

No pain, though. That's something.

Sydney rolled down her driver's window, letting the warm tropical air flow over her face in an attempt to calm her nerves. The car flew up the mostly deserted road to Pearl Harbor, and before she knew it she was pulling into the brushy turnoff she'd scoped out that morning. She cut her headlights and let the vehicle roll into the bushes. Climbing out, she checked her black car from every angle, satisfying herself that no one was likely to spot it. Then she popped the trunk and began preparing for her dive.

All the equipment she'd picked up earlier was neatly arranged, ready to go. Skinning off her clothes, she changed quickly into a full-length black wet suit with a neoprene hood. Then she pulled out the underwater scooter and carried it down to the water's edge. The narrow, mucky strip of beach in front of the mangroves looked different than it had in daylight. Wilder, forsaken, eerie . . .

Shivering, Sydney returned to the car, where she strapped the dive knife to her calf, transferred her waterproof GPS unit and SD-6 telephone into her mesh diving bag, and shrugged into the buoyancy compensator vest supporting her air tank. Depth and pressure gauges were suspended from her vest; her dive light, a wide-lens flashlight with a pistol grip, hung from a loop around her wrist. Grabbing her mask and fins, she closed the car's trunk and pushed its key up inside one tight sleeve of her wet suit.

At the water's edge, Sydney spit into her mask, rubbing saliva around the glass to reduce fogging before bending to rinse it out. Cold water lapped over her bare feet, making her shiver again.

Good thing I went for the full suit, she thought, although her decision to cover herself in black had been based primarily on a desire for invisibility. She seemed to have succeeded on that score; in the darkness of the deserted cove, Sydney could barely see herself. The moon that had lit the sea earlier had waned to the merest ghostly glow, reminding her that she stood near a place where over two thousand men had died terribly. If ghosts actually existed, Pearl Harbor ought to be full of them.

I hope they don't mind my coming, she thought, putting on her mask and securing the dive bag to her waist. *After all, we're on the same side.*

She pulled the battery-powered scooter into waist-deep water, letting it sink lightly to the bottom while she put on her fins. She took the GPS unit from her bag, switched it on, and checked her coordinates. Finally she put the regulator into her mouth, inhaled to make sure it was working, and sank beneath the surface.

Darkness closed around her. She fingered the trigger on the dive light, but decided against turning it on—too visible. Instead, she powered up the scooter, using a Velcro strap to secure the GPS on top where she could see its small glowing display. Gripping the handles on each side of the scooter, she aimed the propeller-driven device out toward the center of the harbor.

She moved slowly at first, unable to see anything in front of her except the GPS screen. When her depth gauge indicated she was ten feet below the surface, she finally flipped on her dive light, pointing the beam forward. Countless tiny particles suspended in the water reflected her light back to her, giving her only a few feet of visibility. Turning the light off again, she increased her scooter speed to two miles per hour, deciding to rely on her reconnaissance of that morning and hope nothing was in her path rather than risk having someone spot a light that was of no use anyway. If she hit anything, the scooter would take the brunt of it.

By the time she reached her mission coordinates, she had grown accustomed to traveling blind, letting the water rushing past her face reassure her that she was still moving. Finally, the correct numbers glowed on her GPS unit. Her waterproof watch indicated that the trip from shore had taken twenty-two minutes. Battery life on the scooter was two hours, and she had at least forty minutes of air left in her tank. So far everything was going like clockwork.

Angling the scooter downward, she cleared her ears and submerged another ten feet, then tried the light again. An organic soup floated past her mask, swallowing the beam so completely that Sydney felt as if she had switched on the bulb inside a closet. Throttling back on the scooter, she glided toward the bottom in a long slow arc, the center of her own tiny capsule of illumination.

She saw the silty bottom only moments before the nose of her scooter would have hit mud. Pulling sharply upward, she avoided the collision but churned up a cloud of sediment that obscured her vision even further. Leveling off, she kept her fins still to avoid stirring up more muck. Within her sphere of light, the bottom was flat and featureless—no coral, no rocks, and definitely no shipwreck. Unfortunately, she could barely see three feet in front of her.

How am I supposed to find anything down here? she wondered despairingly, making a wide circle just feet above the mud. *This would be bad enough during daylight. But now . . .*

The task seemed impossible. She had always known finding the prototype might be tricky; she had foolishly assumed that finding the wreck would be easy. She wished she were working with a partner, someone to help her choose her next move. If Noah were there, he'd have an idea.

At least she wouldn't feel so alone.

Double-checking her GPS coordinates, Sydney made another slow loop. If the *Eagle* was there, she ought to be right on top of it.

So where is it already?

Maybe there wasn't even a wreck to be found. What evidence did Wilson really have, other than an unexplained blip on some top-secret remote sensing survey? If a yacht had really been rusting at the bottom of the harbor for the past sixty years, wouldn't someone have found it by now?

On the other hand, it was common knowledge that there were downed aircraft still on the bottom somewhere. Not everything lost in the war had been found.

A wreck could still be here, she reassured herself, making another, wider loop. *And if it is, I'd better find it.*

She checked her watch again, beginning to worry about her air supply.

Suddenly, her light found something. Rising up from the mud, a heavily encrusted wall sloped steeply away from her, its upper edge disappearing into darkness.

Sydney's heart beat faster. Two swift kicks of her fins propelled her forward as she switched off the scooter, then glided upward along the dark surface until it fell off abruptly beneath her. She angled her light downward—and identified the coral-encrusted deck of a ship lying on its side.

Bingo!

Happiness and relief flooded her equally. Leaving her scooter resting in the ninety-degree angle formed by the steeply tilted deck and a wall enclosing the upper cabin, Sydney began exploring the ship.

Rusted metal cables snaked across the steel deck. Evenly spaced portholes were too overgrown to see through, but one had broken out, leaving a small round hole. Sydney shined her light through it and saw a tiny compartment that might have been a berth.

What had once been the opposite wall of the room was now the floor. Silt covered everything. She could just make out what appeared to be an open interior doorway, but her light didn't penetrate beyond that.

Leaving the porthole, she swam to the aft end of the ship and shined her light on the stern. Beneath a thick coat of rust and algae, faint letters were still visible: EAGLE.

Yes!

Her heart beat even faster with the certainty that she had the right ship, but she forced herself to calm down, knowing her excitement was increasing the load on her air supply. She was still hovering off the stern, trying to regulate her breathing, when a huge bluish fish flashed through the edge of her light, disappearing with one strong sweep of its tail.

Shark!

She froze, unable to think over the terrified roaring of blood in her ears. Had it gone? Was it coming back?

Is it hungry?

The weight in her buoyancy compensator pulled her gently to the bottom until one of her fin blades touched ground. With the exception of the fingers clenching her dive light, every part of her body had gone weak. She wanted to reach down and unstrap her knife, but her arm refused to move. She remained paralyzed on the bottom, shining a trembling light in the direction the shark had gone.

If it's coming back, I at least want to see it. I at least want a chance to fight.

But she still didn't reach for her dive knife. She couldn't help thinking that the moment she averted her eyes, the monster would charge back out of the darkness and snap her in half with one bite. Her chest heaved, wasting air, but she just couldn't make herself budge.

I could go inside the ship. The thought was a ray of hope. *I need to search it anyway. A shark's not going to follow me in there.*

Slowly, cautiously, she pushed up off the mud, barely kicking her feet. The moment she cleared the stern, she headed across the aft deck toward the back of the upper cabin, where she could make out the yawning black hole of an open doorway. She swam slowly toward the opening, every sense on alert.

The rectangle of the doorway was tilted nearly horizontal by the position of the ship. Risking a burst of speed, she darted through it, immediately turning to face open water.

The shark, if it was still out there, had not reappeared to chase her. She had made it. She was safe.

Breathing a sigh of relief, Sydney reached out a hand to steady herself against the doorway.

Calm down, she told herself, taking more deep breaths. *You need to be careful now.*

Diving in shipwrecks was always dangerous,

and no one had been through this one first to re-move the doors and hatches and clear the obstacles. There could be dangling cables, broken glass, jagged metal, dangerous gasses, or other hazards. If she became tangled up somehow, or lost, or if a door latched behind her, she could run out of air and drown. She let her feet sink gently, pulling her upright. One of her fins brushed an interior wall.

Something slammed into her leg, then writhed away from it. Sydney screamed into her regulator, releasing a flurry of bubbles, as a moray eel lunged out of the darkness directly at her mask. The blunt-headed creature's mouth was open, revealing rows of needle-like teeth. Her dive light made mirrors of its bulbous eyes. Six inches from her face it changed direction and shot out the cabin door, dis-appearing into open water.

Sydney choked and sputtered on the water she'd inhaled. The fact that the eel had been as afraid of her as she was of it did little to calm her down.

Was it just cruising through, looking for dinner, or does it live in here? she wondered. *If it lives here, am I going to find more of them?*

One thing was certain: She was going to be a lot more careful where she put her feet.

Turning slowly, she faced the interior of the entry cabin and shined her light around, ready to begin her search. She seemed to be in some sort of navigation center. The wall in front of her contained a bank of instruments mounted at counter height, with a row of encrusted windows above and metal cabinets beneath. Removing her dive knife from its sheath, Sydney pried at the nearest cabinet, only to find it rusted shut.

I should have brought a crowbar, she realized. *And maybe some other tools.*

Abandoning the cabinets, she studied the instrument panel, then began fishing for items tumbled into the silty junction of what had once been the floor and a side wall, doing her best not to stir up the muck and destroy her visibility. She found the hardware from some wooden chairs, a pair of corroded binoculars, and something that might once have been rope—nothing that looked like a nuclear prototype or that could help her bash open a cupboard. She continued searching, going over every bit of the upper cabin, before slipping though a gangway and swimming into the heart of the ship.

The ladder that led to the lower cabins was turned almost sideways now. At what would have been its base, a small galley hung over Sydney's head. Cupboard doors yawned open, the cupboard's contents having spilled some sixty years before. In the thick muck beneath her, Sydney made out the protruding shapes of pots and bottles. Reaching down into their midst, she plucked out a white coffee mug, its rim only slightly chipped. She imagined the man who had used it just going about his business, never suspecting until too late.

Behind the gangway ladder was a closed metal door. Assuming it led to the engine compartment, Sydney decided to try her luck forward, in the passenger cabins. If Suler had been staying on board, the prototype seemed most likely to be there.

Or else in some secret compartment I'll never find without hauling this hulk to the surface and cutting it up with a torch.

Unfortunately, that wasn't how SD-6 did things. Her branch of the CIA didn't concern itself with missions that could be handled in the open.

The doorway to the first cabin on the uphill side of the boat was open, its metal hinges intact, its wooden door disintegrated. Sydney drifted up into the tiny berth, shining her light around. Two narrow metal bunks were affixed to the wall, their mattresses long since rotted away. A narrow locker contained rusted hangers and the soles from several pairs of boots. Anything else that hadn't dissolved had fallen down through the open doorway, piling up with the muck against the opposite side of the central passage. Backing out of the room, Sydney pushed her hand down into the mud a few times, feeling for a stainless-steel case. The ultrafine sediment whirled up around her, clouding the water. She had just decided to move on to the other cabins when a casual glance at her pressure gauge stopped her cold.

That can't be! she thought, stunned.

She was down to her last fifteen minutes of air. She was also forty feet underwater, and even after she swam up to the shallows, the trip back to the beach would take longer than twenty minutes.

Backing up in a panic, Sydney turned and kicked along the ladder into the upper cabin. She hesitated at the doorway, wondering if the shark was still cruising around outside, but there was no time left to wait and see. Mustering her courage, she bolted out into open water and swam to her scooter. Checking the GPS unit, she memorized the true, adjusted wreck coordinates. Then, steeling herself for the worst, she switched off her dive light.

The scooter pulled her swiftly through the darkness. Sydney kept her angle low, climbing gradually to achieve maximum forward movement. She hadn't been deep enough long enough to worry about decompression, but she needed to conserve each precious second of air. She kept her body as still as possible, relying on the scooter, but her mind was in total chaos.

How did I use up my air so fast?

It didn't seem possible. The only thing she could think of was that the combination of fear and exertion had caused her to use her supply at a greatly accelerated rate.

Or there's something wrong with the tank. Or the regulator. Or the gauge.

There was always a risk with new equipment. But bringing her own from L.A. had been out of the question. Besides, she had checked everything herself.

Sydney consulted her gauges; she was ten feet below the surface, with maybe ten minutes more of air. Her GPS unit put her fifteen minutes off the beach. If she had worn her snorkel, she could have cruised just under the surface with only its tube above water, but she had foolishly decided she didn't need one.

She was going to have to surface for the last part of her journey. She didn't see any way around it.

Two hundred yards off the beach, Sydney's air ran out. She took her last breath and held it, angling the scooter up toward the surface. She didn't have to swim. If she could just hold on for the next five or six minutes without passing out . . .

She didn't make it. Fifty yards off the beach, she cut the scooter's power and broke the surface. She treaded water, refilling her lungs, then sank a couple of feet and began swimming toward the beach, pushing the scooter in front of her. At last she reached the shallows. Ditching the scooter on the bottom, she eased her head into the air.

The night was dark, but after the blackness underwater, she found she could see pretty well. The shoreline was sharp, especially the narrow strip in front of the mangroves, but the trees themselves were a bank of shadows. Sydney removed her fins and planted her feet on the muddy bottom. She had just begun to stand when a flash of movement caught her eye.

Someone was hiding in the trees.

She froze, then slowly lowered herself back into the water, her gaze fixed on the mangroves. A twig snapped near the edge of the grove.

And then she saw it—the back of a blond head dashing away toward the road.

Ashley!

Sydney didn't know whether to give chase or stay where she was and hope she hadn't been recognized.

But if Ashley doesn't know about me, what is she doing here?

Forgetting about stealth, Sydney charged out of the water, shrugging off equipment as she ran. She was only halfway to the road when she heard an engine start. Increasing her pace to a sprint, she arrived just in time to see a car pull onto the pavement and roar off toward Honolulu—no lights, no license plate. Sydney couldn't even tell for sure what make the vehicle was.

That's it, she thought, sick at heart. *If my cover wasn't blown before, it's totally shattered now.*

8

SYDNEY HAD TO COLLECT her diving gear before she could leave the harbor. Then she lost more precious time examining her rental car for bombs, bugs, and other signs of Ashley's presence. Finally, she called Wilson.

"I think I'm in trouble," she whispered, sinking low in the driver's seat. The car was stuffy, but she kept the windows up, paranoid about being overheard.

"What kind of trouble?" Even at that early hour, Wilson's voice crackled intensely, as if he'd already downed two pots of coffee. "What's our status?"

"I don't have the package."

"Why not?"

"I verified your survey. But as far as the item of interest goes . . . I had some technical problems."

"So is it there or not?"

"I don't know."

Wilson sighed impatiently.

"It gets worse," she told him. "I think my cover's blown."

"You *think*?"

"It's blown," she admitted miserably. "This has been the worst night ever! First, we had to go on this stupid dinner cruise, and I thought Francie—"

"Do I have time for this?" he interrupted harshly. "Who ID'ed you?"

"Her name is Ashley Evans. She's in the sorority."

"Who does she work for?"

"I don't know."

"What the hell *do* you know?" he exploded. "I send you out to complete a mission, and so far all you're doing is whining."

Sydney sucked in her breath, wounded.

"I don't even know why you're calling," he said. "If this Ashley is a threat, you know what you have to do."

She hesitated.

"Right?" He sounded two seconds short of blowing a vein.

"Right," she agreed quickly. "I'll take care of it."

Wilson hung up. Sydney tossed the phone into

the passenger seat and backed the car out of the bushes, tears stinging her eyes. She had thought of Wilson as a second father—tough, but kind. There had been nothing kind about that phone call.

All I wanted was advice, she thought, pulling onto the road without checking for traffic. *I didn't need him to go off on me.*

And how, exactly, did he expect her to deal with Ashley? She had said she'd take care of it, but she didn't have the first clue what that entailed.

Except that he'd made it sound kind of ominous.

He can't be suggesting I hurt her.

Can he?

For a moment, Sydney forgot to steer. Her wheels drifted over a row of reflector bumps, the sudden thumping snapping her back to her senses.

Of course not! He probably meant I should keep an eye on Ashley. Find out who she works for.

There was only one problem with that plan.

First she had to *find* Ashley.

* * *

There was no sign of Ashley in the hotel lobby. There was no sign of anyone, except a single yawning front-desk clerk. The lack of activity was hardly surprising at that hour; after all she had been through, it was a miracle Sydney was still awake.

Only adrenaline was keeping her going—but she was still buzzing with that.

She had driven through Chinatown on her way back, hoping to find Ashley at the warehouse. No one had been there, though, and after staking it out a few minutes, Sydney had decided to check the hotel. She had parked her rental car in a different garage—just in case—and walked nearly a mile to the Waikiki Princess. Now she hesitated in the lobby, wondering whether she should approach the clerk about Ashley's whereabouts. Would he know if she was in her room?

She had begun to walk toward the desk when a sudden noise behind her made her whirl around.

"Surprise!" Noah cried, grinning from ear to ear.

Tired, scared, and frustrated, Sydney lashed out without thinking. "You have *got* to stop sneaking up on me! A guy could get killed that way."

Noah's smile dimmed. "I'll take my chances."

"I don't like your odds. What are you doing here, anyway?"

He was wearing red shorts, flip-flops, and the loudest flowered shirt on Oahu. If his cover was the world's most color-blind tourist, he had it totally nailed.

"I thought you'd be happy to see me," he said. "Obviously, I was wrong."

She stared, trying to understand.

"Did Wilson send you? Because if he did I'll—"

"Maybe we can talk outside," Noah interrupted.

Grabbing her by the arm, he propelled her through the open-air lobby, out onto the first terrace.

"Are you crazy?" he whispered. "Dropping names in public?" Stars winked overhead and a slight breeze rustled the palms, but neither Noah nor Sydney noticed the romantic setting. "What's the matter with you?"

"I'm having a bad night."

"Thanks for making it mutual."

His words drew her up short, making her feel guilty on top of everything else.

"I'm sorry, all right? You just couldn't have caught me at a worse time."

Noah looked offended. "It didn't sound like a bad time on the phone this afternoon."

"Things were different then!" Even she could hear the shrewish edge to her voice. She took a slow, deep breath. "Listen, do you want to go sit by the swimming pool?"

"Do you?"

The boyish smile had vanished, replaced by his usual cautious expression. She had caused that, she knew, but she was too tired to repair the damage. Leading the way down to the glowing pool, she selected a double lounge chair at the farthest edge of the deck. There, sitting next to Noah in the shadow of the immaculate landscaping, she tried to explain.

"My mission's in the toilet," she said, twisting around to see his face. "But since you're here, I assume you know that."

"Sydney, I came to see *you*. I don't even know what your mission is."

"You . . . What?"

"I took some personal time. After we talked on the phone, I started thinking about how nice a few days in the islands would be, and how maybe you and I could spend some time together. But if your mission is in trouble . . . What's going on?"

"It's nothing. You really came to see me?"

He shrugged. "When I devised that brilliant plan, it seemed like a good idea. It could have been those beers I had with lunch."

"No. It's sweet." She reached to touch his knee, then chickened out.

"So what's the story here? What's the problem with your mission?"

"It's nothing," she lied again, not wanting to look like a loser. "I'll take care of it."

"But if you thought Wilson sent me . . . Does he know there's a snag?"

"Yes. He knows all about it," she said tensely.

"And what did he say to do?"

"He said to handle it, and I will. What ever happened to 'just here to see Sydney'?"

"Did it occur to you that I might be able to help?"

"I don't need any help, Noah."

That was the biggest lie of all. She'd have jumped on the offer of assistance from anyone else in SD-6. She just couldn't stand to fail in front of him.

"Okay," he said coolly. "If you don't want to trust me, that's your call."

"It's not that I don't *trust* you."

"No, forget it." He was way more offended than necessary. "Forgive me for even asking."

"Don't be like that."

"Like what? How am I being, Sydney?"

"The same as always!" she said, exasperated. "It's all about the mission with you. It's *always* about the mission. It's *only* about the mission."

"Is that so?" His voice was a mile away. "If that's how you feel, then maybe I'd better leave."

Tears welled up to her lashes. The lump in her throat hurt so much she could barely breathe. She nodded once, then closed her eyes.

"Maybe you'd better," she said.

The chair rebounded as Noah stood up. There were no good-byes, no parting words, only the sound of his flip-flops retreating across the concrete.

She listened until she was sure he had gone.

Then she finally let herself cry.

This has been the worst night of my life!

In the past few hours, she'd blown her mission,

her cover, and any chance she'd ever have with Noah.

Wilson was mad at her.

Ashley was in hiding somewhere, probably trying to figure out how to kill her.

Even Francie, her supposed best friend, was down on her for jumping off that stupid boat.

And who cares if she wasn't actually in the water? Hasn't she ever heard of gratitude?

Sydney choked back a long, shuddering sob. Francie would come around eventually. But Noah . . .

Is he ever going to speak to me again?

Hunched over on the hotel lounge chair, tears running down her face, Sydney felt completely, utterly abandoned. With SD-6, college, and now AKX, she had never had more people in her life.

So how come I feel so alone?

"ARE YOU GETTING UP, or what?"

Francie's voice came through to Sydney like another part of her fractured dream. She was swimming, swimming, swimming . . . but was she getting anywhere? Her legs felt like lead, and everything was so dark. . . .

"Fine. I'm going to breakfast without you."

The slam of their hotel room door jolted Sydney bolt upright. She fell back into bed, groaning as a shaft of sunlight found her swollen eyes. Her body was sore, her emotions raw, her head throbbing. She felt like she was hungover, without any of the fun beforehand.

Forcing herself to sit up again, she double-checked the clock on the nightstand. How could it be ten in the morning? That would mean she'd had five hours of sleep, but she felt like she'd just closed her eyes. She swung her feet down to the carpet and tottered to the window, nearly tripping over a potted silk orchid as she drew the curtains wide.

Waikiki Beach spread in front of her. Already the sparkling sand was dotted with towels, the aqua water so clear she could see straight to the bottom. The sunny scene was surreal compared to the darkness in her head.

Her failures of the night before consumed her, not one of them resolved. Even Francie was still mad. Meanwhile, she had an enemy agent to deal with and a nuclear prototype to find. Moaning, she headed for the shower.

The hot water revived her somewhat, and by the time she had dressed to go downstairs her brain was working again. She'd ask around to see if anyone knew where Ashley was; then she'd make an excuse to Roxy and head off on her own.

I have to take that dive gear in and get my tank refilled. And I'd better switch rental cars first— Ashley had way too much time with the old one.

Sydney wondered again about the men she had seen Ashley meet, both in the warehouse and on the cruise. If Ashley was working with a team, anyone could be following Sydney and she might not even know it. Once again, she felt her disadvantage.

If I'd let Noah help me, I'd have a team too.

Sydney shook her head, unable to believe her own stupidity.

At least I've got my pride, she told herself sarcastically.

The sisters were scheduled to eat breakfast on their own that morning. Sydney headed for the hotel restaurant, hoping she wasn't the only girl who'd slept in. With luck, she'd be able to pick up some eggs and news of Ashley at the same time. Maybe someone had seen her leave the night before, or knew where she'd gone since.

To Sydney's complete amazement, Ashley herself was sitting at a corner table with Gretchen, wearing dark glasses and looking like something the tide had washed up. It was shocking to see her at all, let alone to see her so wrecked.

And then Sydney remembered.

Right, she thought slowly. *All that pretend drinking on the boat. Today she's got a pretend hangover.*

They were going to finish this game of cat-and-mouse in public, then. Abruptly, Sydney remembered something Noah had said at a crucial point in their Paris mission: "We got this far in one piece, so they must not be sure about us."

Could that be the case here, too? After everything

that had happened, Sydney found it hard to believe that Ashley wasn't sure about her. Maybe something else was holding her back.

The mission! she realized in a rush. *She still doesn't know what my mission is!*

Not only that, but Ashley probably still believed that her own cover was secure. It was the first positive thought Sydney had had in hours. She was down, but she wasn't out. Not yet.

Floating on the high of her new knowledge, Sydney walked directly to Ashley's table.

"Hey, Sydney!" Gretchen greeted her. "You look dry this morning."

"Right." Sydney smiled, letting the gibe roll off her. "It's all good now. But how about you, Ashley? If I didn't know better, I'd say you'd had a rough night."

Ashley barely glanced at her. "Whatever," she said muzzily, turning her gaze out the window.

The girl's acting skills were top-notch—Sydney had to give her that. She stood there a moment longer, trying to think of some way to draw Ashley out, before deciding to leave well enough alone. They were on to each other, and now they *both* knew it.

Leaving Ashley, Sydney crossed to the other side of the dining room, where she'd spotted an empty table. She was just about to sit when Roxy hailed her from the far corner.

"Sydney! Hey, Syd! There you are!"

Roxy's hair was wound into a smooth French twist set off with a white plumeria. She looked like the perfect island girl as she stood and motioned for Sydney to join her at a booth.

"Are you eating by yourself this morning too?" Sydney asked, sliding into the bench across from Roxy. There were dirty dishes on the table, but the only thing in front of Roxy was an umbrella-topped glass of iced tea.

"Nah. Keisha was here earlier. And Francie. Hey, tell me if it's none of my business . . . but are you two having some kind of fight?"

From someone else, Sydney might have resented the question, but Roxy looked so genuinely concerned that she found herself explaining.

"Not really," she said, with a roll of her eyes. "She's just mad because I jumped off the boat and scared her. It's all pretty stupid."

"Wow," said Roxy, shaking her head. "You'd think she'd be grateful you care. I mean, you *were* trying to save her life."

"Exactly! Thank you!" At least somebody understood.

"I'm going to lie out by the pool today, if you want to hang with me," Roxy offered. "We have a pretty loose day, schedule-wise."

"Thanks. I might take you up on that."

She was still trying to decide how best to inform

Roxy of her impending absence when the waitress appeared. Starving from the night before, Sydney ordered macadamia nut pancakes, scrambled eggs, bacon, and a side of fruit.

"How *do* you keep your girlish figure?" Roxy teased when the woman left.

"Exercise," Sydney told her truthfully.

"You'll have to forgive me if I don't stick around to watch you eat," said Roxy, pushing her glass away. "I promised my mom I'd call her this morning, and now's the perfect time."

"Go ahead," Sydney urged. "I'm fine on my own."

Roxy glanced across the dining room, then smiled. "I don't think you'll be alone for long. Catch you later, Syd."

She slipped away just moments before Francie appeared at the table, plunking into Roxy's warm seat and staring at Sydney accusingly.

"I, uh . . . thought you already ate," Sydney said awkwardly.

"I did."

"Oh."

Sydney glanced toward Ashley's corner of the restaurant. The girl was still there, her blond head visible over the back of the booth.

"What you did last night was crazy," said Francie. "You could have been killed jumping off that boat."

"We already covered this. I thought you were in

the water, and that's the only reason I did it. I'm sorry I embarrassed you."

"Embarrassed?" Tears quivered in Francie's eyes. She tried to blink them back, but they spilled over anyway, dropping onto the tablecloth. "Did you ever stop to think how I'd feel if you died? Or w-w-worse," she stammered on a rising sob, "if you died, and it was my fault?"

"Francie!" Sydney moved quickly around the table to give her friend a reassuring hug. "I'm not going to die." The promise made her remember Ashley, but the girl was behind her now, out of sight. "Or, if I do," she amended, "it won't be your fault."

"It was my fault you jumped into the ocean."

"No, it was Ashley's. That girl's a lunatic."

Francie managed a smile. "You don't like her?"

"Honestly? I can't stand her. So if you happen to see me push her into a live volcano or something, I hope you won't hold it against me."

She couldn't tell Francie she was only half kidding.

Francie laughed happily. "There aren't any live volcanoes on Oahu. You'd have to go to the Big Island for that."

Sydney pretended to consider. "Okay. It'll be worth the trip," she said, setting Francie laughing again.

The waitress reappeared with breakfast and began putting down plates.

"Excuse me, but I didn't order hash browns," Sydney told her.

"No? I'm sorry." The woman reached to take them back.

"What she *means* is," Francie put in hurriedly, "can we get some catsup with those?"

Sydney smiled and handed her friend a fork.

*   *   *

By the time Sydney finished breakfast, Katie and Michelle had joined them and were deep in conversation with Francie about the celebrities they'd seen on their last trip to Cannes.

"I'm going up to the room," Sydney interrupted, restless at the thought of everything she still had to do.

Francie waved her off. "I'll be there in a minute."

The moment Sydney stood up, she noticed that Ashley was gone, her table now occupied by an elderly couple. She felt an anxious twinge, then let it go. It wasn't as if she could watch the girl every second anyway—she had things of her own to take care of.

Riding the elevator up to her room, Sydney made her plans. She'd change clothes and leave a note telling Francie she'd gone for a run—that ought to cover her long enough to swap rental cars and take care of her equipment for later that night. She'd be back in time to meet Roxy at the pool, and no one would ever even know she was gone.

She opened her door, ready to hurry, then stopped and stared in disbelief.

The sheets and blankets from both beds had been stripped and were in a heap on the floor. Sydney's clothes looked as if they'd exploded out of her suitcase, flinging themselves all over the room. Francie's suitcase had been dumped on the floor, and the dresses in the closet were all off their hangers. Shoes had been tossed around as if scattered by a tornado.

Sydney half hoped to find Ashley hiding in the bathroom, so they could settle things right there. But while her toiletries were all over the floor, Sydney's rival spy was long gone.

Sydney slapped a Do Not Disturb sign on the doorknob. She flipped the security bolt so Francie wouldn't be able to get in, then hurried to the closet, straightening dresses and returning shoes, each movement quick and methodical. Next she tackled Francie's suitcase, taking pains to refold and replace things exactly as they had been, hoping to get it right.

At least I know Ashley didn't steal anything.

The only spy equipment that wasn't in the rental car was Sydney's SD-6 cell phone, and she'd been carrying that, just in case Wilson called.

The main thing right now is to keep Francie

from guessing what happened. She'd go nuts if she knew about this!

Especially as Sydney had no intention of ever reporting the break-in.

Finishing with Francie's suitcase, she moved to her own, putting things back without worrying too much about neatness. She folded the blankets and put them on the beds, piling the sheets beside them.

If the maid doesn't beat Francie in here, I'll say I just wanted to make sure they changed the sheets.

It wasn't as good as remaking the beds herself, but she had more important things to do, like sort out the mess in the bathroom.

Picking up the lipsticks and makeup brushes on the floor, trying to separate her things from Francie's, Sydney wondered what Ashley thought she was going to find in their cosmetic bags. *Bugs, maybe. Minicams. Tracking devices. Microfilm.* Actually, there were a lot of possibilities—if a person didn't know what she was looking for.

And that was when it hit her: *If I'd found the prototype last night, Ashley would have it right now!*

The thought rocked her far worse than the mess in her room. Every time she thought she had Ashley figured out, the girl went another way. She had never expected burglary, and certainly not in broad daylight.

I could have walked in on her. Francie could have walked in on her.

A chill ran between Sydney's shoulders. What if Francie had confronted Ashley?

For the second time in as many days, she was afraid for her best friend's life.

The problem is, what am I going to do about it?

* * *

Sydney found Roxy already at the swimming pool. The redhead was lounging in her blue bikini, reading a novel with a busty woman and a pirate on its cover. She put it aside when she saw Sydney, but her welcoming smile quickly turned to a look of confusion.

"Where's your bathing suit?" she asked.

Sydney had left a note for Francie and was now wearing running clothes.

"Something's happened," she said in a low voice, perching on the edge of the lounge next to Roxy's. "Somebody's been in my room."

Roxy's brows drew together. "Like the maid?"

"No. Definitely not the maid. Someone was, uh . . . in my things." She was taking a huge risk telling Roxy any of this; it might be better not to get too detailed.

Roxy sat up. "Is anything missing?"

"No."

"There you go, then!" she said, smiling. "It was probably *menehunes*."

"Many whaties?"

"This guy told me about them on the cruise last night. *Menehunes* are these mischievous little locals, always getting into stuff. Kind of like Hawaiian leprechauns."

Sydney took a deep breath. Obviously she had played things down *too* far.

"No, listen, Roxy. This is serious." She glanced around to make extra sure no one was listening. "I think it was Ashley."

"Ashley?" Roxy's blue eyes went wide. "Why would Ashley go into your room?"

"I can't say." That much was certainly true. "Maybe she was looking for something to steal."

"Like what?"

"Jewelry, money. I don't know."

"But that's crazy!" Roxy protested. "Ashley's folks are loaded."

"Sometimes . . . people have secrets. You think you know someone, but—"

"We should get Security," Roxy interrupted, jumping to her feet. "They'll find out who did it."

"No!"

Roxy froze, an incredulous look on her face.

"I mean, I'd rather keep this among the sisters. Wouldn't you?"

"I guess so," Roxy said slowly. "But what if it *isn't* Ashley? What if it's some total stranger?"

"It's Ashley," Sydney insisted. "I can't tell you how I know. I just do."

Roxy settled back onto her lounge chair, stunned. "Nothing like this has ever happened in AKX before. I mean, we're *better* than that. You know?"

"I know," Sydney assured her. "It's just . . . could you help me keep an eye on Ashley? And on my room? I don't want to tell Francie, because I don't want her to worry. And I can't confront Ashley, because I don't have any proof. But if you could help me watch her . . ."

Roxy nodded, still a little dazed but starting to come around. "Definitely. I'm on it. I'll watch that girl like a hawk."

"That would be great." Sydney played her final card. "I was going to take a long run, get this all out of my system. But if you think I ought to hang around . . ."

"No, go." Roxy stood up. "I'll wander around and see what everyone else is up to. I think I just remembered an AKX project that will keep Ashley busy all day." She smiled conspiratorially. "At least, I will have by the time I find her."

Sydney's return smile was straight from her heart. "Thanks, Roxy. You're the best."

Roxy laughed, the motion jiggling the jewel in her navel. "I am, aren't I? Be sure to spread that around."

10

AT THE COVE IN Pearl Harbor for the second night, Sydney glanced over her shoulder at every sound. She'd arrived earlier than the night before, giving herself more moon to work with. But the same moonlight that allowed her to see what she was doing as she prepared for her dive also allowed others to see her. It was a huge relief to finally sink beneath the dark water en route to the wreck site.

Her scooter towed her quietly, the GPS unit still her only guide. But this time she had precise coordinates—and she knew what to expect. A newly purchased crowbar, hammer, and set of bolt cutters swung heavily in the dive bag at her waist. She'd be ready to open anything now, and she was determined to finish searching the entire ship this time. Maybe the prototype was down there, maybe not. Either way, she wanted to be sure without making a third dive.

When her coordinates put her over the wreck site, Sydney dove swiftly, pausing only to equalize the pressure in her ears and switch on her dive light. Ditching the scooter in the same spot on deck, she swam toward the stern of the *Eagle,* determined not to think about sharks. She paused at the tilted cabin doorway just long enough to check for eels, then swam quickly inside.

Under the instrument panel, the bank of cabinets that had defeated her knife offered little resistance to a heavy-duty crowbar. She popped open the first set of doors, but found nothing of interest inside. Perhaps the compartment had once held charts; all that remained was sludge. Moving down the row, Sydney continued opening and inspecting cabinets. She found the rubberized remains of some foul-weather gear. At one point, the discovery of a decaying box made her heart race, but all it contained was a ruined sextant for celestial navigation.

Convinced she had thoroughly searched the upper cabin, she made her way belowdecks. She had already checked the galley and first tiny berth overhead. Now she decided to start at the bow, in the forwardmost chamber of the ship, and work her way back from there. If she didn't find the proto-type by the time she'd returned to the galley, she'd check the aft engine compartment.

As soon as Sydney entered the V-berth of the *Eagle,* something told her she was in the right place. This compartment was far more luxurious than the other berth, as if fitted out for the captain—or his important guests. The entire chamber had probably once been paneled in wood, although only worm-eaten remnants remained. The brass fixtures were badly corroded. A small metal table was bolted to the steeply angled floor, and a large raised platform filled the narrowest point of the cabin, extending out into the room. Sydney recognized it as the base of a bed and drifted over for a closer look. The mattress had rotted, leaving a set of rusted springs still at-tached to the metal structure. And on both sides of the platform were drawers—locked steel drawers.

If it were me, I'd keep anything important right here, Sydney thought, whipping out her crowbar again. Under the bed might not be the most original hiding place, but Dr. Suler couldn't have predicted the events that had unfolded. He wouldn't have had much time. Forcing the bar down behind the first drawer front, Sydney jimmied it forward, destroying the cor-roded lock and breaking off a rusted slab of metal.

Shining her dive light into the hole she'd cre-ated, Sydney peered in behind it. Nothing.

Undeterred, she pried open the next drawer, and the next. Still nothing.

There were three more drawers on the downhill side of the pedestal. Sydney pulled them apart too, working faster and faster as each one yielded only sludge. Her heart sank as she peered into the last one.

Nothing.

She checked a wall locker with no success and was about to leave the room when a new idea seized her. Swimming back to the bed pedestal, she wedged her crowbar under a thick section of the metal springs on top and jimmied them with all her strength. The springs broke off and fell away, taking enough rusted metal with them to make a small hole near the center top of the platform. Muck billowed up from where the springs landed, but not enough to blind her. Working with the bar, Sydney pulled and pried and shoved, enlarging the opening until she had a good-sized hole. Shining her light into it, she caught her breath with joy. As she had guessed, the drawers on the sides of the pedestal didn't occupy the entire width of the bed. There was an empty space between their opposing backs, enough room for someone to pull a drawer completely out and hide something behind it. And there, dulled but not destroyed by sixty years in salt water, was a lunchbox-sized stainless-steel case.

She reached for it eagerly, full of hope. Wiping

away the layer of scum near its handle, she found three initials on an inlaid gold plaque: BLS.

Got it! she thought triumphantly.

She quickly removed the hammer and bolt cutters from her dive bag and dropped them with the crowbar to make room for the prototype. She stowed the precious case with her SD-6 phone, made sure the mesh bag was securely closed, and reattached it to her waist. Then, anxious to get her find to dry land, she turned and swam for the exit.

Gliding back down the central passage, Sydney floated through the galley, then kicked her way along the ladder into the upper cabin. With her light held out in front of her, she headed directly for the tilted exit doorway. In her mind, she was already back on the scooter, on her way to the beach. She was totally unprepared when something slammed into her tank from behind.

The clanging blow knocked Sydney sideways, nearly forcing the regulator from her mouth. Spinning around, she caught only a glimpse of a gloved hand as it brought a metal bar down across her outstretched forearm. Pain seared up to her shoulder. Her dropped light spiraled to the floor as her attacker came at her again, grabbing for her dive bag.

Reacting instinctively, Sydney punched the heel of her hand at her attacker's head. She could see only a silhouette, and that just barely, but she felt her blow connect, snapping the other diver's head back. The impact pushed them away from each other. Sydney lunged for the knife on her calf, freeing it from its sheath and holding it in front of her as she backed out the doorway into open water.

Outside the cabin, she was plunged into darkness, forced to feel her way along the cabin roof toward her scooter. She was halfway there when the darkness suddenly lifted. The other diver had the light and was swimming up behind her. Squinting into the beam, Sydney lunged with her knife, slashing blindly. She connected with the barrel of the light just as the metal bar crashed into her arm again. The knife and light were dropped simultaneously, fluttering down through the water.

Sydney hesitated, then attacked, both hands groping for contact. Her fingers touched neoprene, then lost it again as an arm twisted out of her grip. She felt the swish of the bar as it grazed past her mask, barely missing her face. She grabbed automatically, this time capturing the arm with the weapon and twisting it hard. On land, the move would have dislocated her opponent's shoulder; now she simply spun the other diver around. Pushing the trapped arm up high, Sydney removed the bar from a weakened hand and pulled it back, ready to strike.

Her instincts revolted at the thought of landing the blow from behind, like an executioner. She couldn't even see the person she'd be hitting, but based on size and physical strength, she felt certain her attacker was a woman. Sydney let the weapon drop; then, in almost the same motion, she reached forward and grabbed her opponent's air hose, yanking sharply. An eruption of bubbles rushed past her face as the hose broke free somewhere. The other diver struggled desperately. Curling her legs in front of her, Sydney put her fins on her opponent's back and pushed hard, forcing her away into darkness. Quickly, before her enemy could recover, Sydney found the cabin roof and felt her way back to where she'd left the scooter.

To her relief, the vehicle was still there, its guiding GPS unit still attached. Sydney switched on its propeller and pushed away from the *Eagle,* revving the scooter to full power. At just over two miles per hour, she wasn't setting any speed records, but no swimmer would be able to catch her.

Assuming anyone's still swimming.

Sydney wasn't sure how much damage she'd done to the other diver's air supply, but there was no doubt she'd caused a major problem. Whether it could be fixed, in total darkness, on one last breath of air, was something she didn't much want to think about.

It was self-defense, she reminded herself. *Whoever that was obviously wanted the prototype at all costs.*

But there was little real doubt in Sydney's mind as to the identity of the other diver.

Ashley. Who else?

Back at the beach, Sydney cut the power to her scooter and glided into a different part of the cove. There had been no sign of pursuit, but she couldn't rule out the possibility of backup lying in wait on the shore. Poking her head just above the water, Sydney scanned the deserted beach, looking for signs of surveillance. She'd gone through far too much to have the prototype taken from her now.

At last she decided she had to move. Kicking silently the rest of the way to shore, she quickly removed her fins, depositing them and the scooter just above the waterline. She shrugged off her tank there too, and dropped her mask beside it. Then she crept cautiously past the mangroves, ready to fight if necessary.

Nothing moved in the trees. Seeing no one, Sydney continued up the slope to the brushy turnoff. There was no sign her car had been touched, not a trace of a suspicious footstep on the dusty ground around it. Suddenly Sydney remembered there ought to be a second car somewhere—Ashley's car. Hurrying up to the roadside where Ashley had peeled out before, Sydney found nothing. No car, no fresh tire tracks. Barefoot and cold in her soaked wet suit, she circled the area, looking for clues. She found no indication that anyone else had been there recently.

Walking back to the shore, Sydney stood in the shadow of the mangroves and looked out over the harbor. Moonlight glinted off tiny ripples, but no diver appeared. Once again, Sydney wondered if Ashley had drowned.

I could have made it to the surface, she thought. *Forty feet isn't that far.*

On the other hand, she'd been practicing holding her breath ever since her Paris mission, whereas Ashley would have been kicked short of air, disoriented, and abandoned in total darkness.

Which is her own fault! Sydney thought, not liking how guilty she felt.

She carried her dive gear up to her car and stashed it in the trunk, then quickly stripped off her wet suit and pulled on some dry clothes. Removing the prototype and cell phone from her dive bag, Sydney shut the trunk and opened the driver's door, locking herself in the car.

Feeling slightly more secure, she flipped on a tiny flashlight, getting her first good look at the prototype case.

The case itself was in perfect condition, but the lock beneath the handle was corroded and would have to be broken. Not only that, but there was some sort of corrosion around the junction between the two halves, effectively welding them shut. Switching the light back off, Sydney dialed her boss.

"Wilson here." The way he barked the words made her wonder if he ever slept.

"It's Sydney. I've got it," she whispered back, still worried about being overheard.

"That's better!" His voice was so full of warmth again that she could almost hear him smiling. "How does it look?"

"Amazingly clean. Like he had it coated with some sort of miracle growth repellent."

"Anything's possible. Is it intact?"

"And locked. Do you want me to break it open?"

"No," he said quickly. "It's better to do that in the lab. Is there water inside it?"

Sydney shook the case next to her ear.

"I don't hear anything, and it's sealed all the way around. I think it's exactly the way he left it."

"Fantastic!" said Wilson. "I knew you could do it!"

"Yeah, well . . . the problem is, what do I do with it now? Ashley and I fought on the wreck, and I don't know where she went."

"I thought you were going to take care of Ashley."

"I may have just taken care of her permanently. I haven't seen her come up."

There was a pause while Wilson considered that information.

"You should know Ashley Evans is an alias," he said. "We're still looking, but so far this girl doesn't exist before college. Deep cover—I doubt that surprises you."

"Nothing about Ashley surprises me. Listen, Wilson. I can't keep the prototype at the hotel. My room's already been broken into once, and I don't trust the hotel safe, considering what I'm dealing with here. I know you planned for me to ship it to you, but that would be crazy now. I don't know who's watching me. I don't know who's listening. The only thing I know for sure is that someone will try to steal this thing the second it's out of my hands."

"Agreed," said Wilson. "You'll have to hang on to it."

"But there's no way I can bring it back on the plane! If I check it in my luggage, we'll never see that suitcase again, and if I try to carry it aboard . . . We can't risk having it confiscated."

"No."

"So what am I supposed to do?"

"Give me a couple of days," he said. "I have a boat working a recovery mission northwest of you. I think I can get it to Honolulu for a handoff Wednesday night."

"Wednesday? But this is only Monday! What am I supposed to do until then?"

"Three things. Keep the prototype with you at all times. Guard it with your life. And stay alive."

"MAN. THAT'S A LONG way down," said Francie, standing beside Sydney at the edge of the sheer cliff. "I wouldn't want to fall."

"If you did, you'd probably be blown right back up," Sydney said, shouting to be heard above the howling wind.

"It didn't work for those Hawaiian guys," Francie pointed out.

Sydney laughed, but she was feeling anything but lighthearted. The entire sorority was taking a private limo-bus tour that Tuesday, and their current location was the Nuuanu Pali lookout, a spot high in the mountainous center of southern Oahu. Although only a short drive from Waikiki, the cliff the girls were standing on seemed incredibly wild and remote. The wind wailed eerily in Sydney's ears, recalling the tour guide's tale of the native warriors Kamehameha the Great had driven off the clifftop long ago in his bid to conquer the island. Far below the steep green hillsides, the towns on the distant windward shoreline looked like toys. The blue Pacific sparkled beyond them, its whitecaps a sprinkling of sugar. The beauty of the place was breathtaking, but there were only two things on Sydney's mind: the prototype in her backpack, and the fact that Ashley was standing at the edge of the cliff not fifty feet away.

She had been stunned to see Ashley climb aboard the bus earlier that morning, acting as if it were just another day. But despite everything that had happened between them, Sydney was glad she hadn't killed her.

Not that I wouldn't, if she forced me to. Her eyes drifted Ashley's way again.

As if reading her mind, Ashley looked up from the view, her gaze locking with Sydney's. Open hostility flashed between them, so intense that Sydney was surprised everyone didn't feel it. But the other girls continued chatting and pointing out landmarks, completely oblivious.

"I'm going back to the bus," Francie announced. "I think I left my sunglasses on the seat."

Sydney nodded distractedly, her attention still on Ashley. With one last hateful glare, her enemy turned and moved away to the very edge of the cliff, so close that Sydney imagined a sudden, shifting gust of wind blowing her right over.

Which might not be such a bad thing, she mused. So long as Ashley's death wasn't on her conscience, it was hard to deny its advantages.

My cover would be secure again. I wouldn't have to worry every second about someone sneaking up behind me trying to snag the prototype. I'd—

"Whoa!"

An unexpected hand on her shoulder made Sydney shout and wheel around, her pulse in overdrive.

But, to her embarrassment, the hand belonged to Roxy.

"What were you daydreaming about?" Roxy asked, laughing. "You act like I'm trying to push you off!"

*   *   *

"Agent Hicks isn't in," a cold female voice informed Sydney, "and I'm not authorized to discuss his whereabouts."

"I wasn't asking for his *whereabouts,*" Sydney objected lamely. "I only wanted to know—"

"I'm not authorized to discuss *anything* regarding

Agent Hicks," the SD-6 operator interrupted. "You may leave a message, or not. That's all."

I suppose asking for his cell phone number is out of the question. But Sydney couldn't find the nerve to say that. She was already dangerously close to sounding pathetic.

"No message," she said, and hung up. The last thing she needed was to start a rumor flying around headquarters.

Dropping the phone into her lap, she looked out on a perfect Waikiki sunset and sighed. She had finally managed to separate herself and her backpack from the rest of the sorority, walking way down the beach in order to make her secret phone call. Maybe it was risky to let Ashley out of her sight, but she couldn't stop thinking about Noah.

If I'd accepted his help instead of acting like such a baby, there'd be two of us guarding this proto- type now. Or I could have handed it off to him and just been done with it.

But that wasn't the reason she wanted to talk to him. Ever since he'd left, she hadn't been able to get him out of her mind.

I can't leave things the way they are, she thought, blind to the gorgeous scenery. *I have to apologize, even if he never forgives me.*

She wasn't even sure he should. After everything he'd said about the dangers of agents developing close relationships, it must have been nearly impossible for him to admit there might be *anything* between them. And instead of seizing the opportunity, she had stomped on his feelings like . . . like . . .

Like a spoiled sorority girl, she thought, depressed.

"There you are!" Francie's voice rang out across the beach, startling Sydney back to the present. "What are you doing way down here?"

"Just, uh . . . hanging out. Watching the sunset. What are *you* doing here?"

"Looking for you." Francie plopped down cross-legged in the sand. "I didn't know where—" She broke off in midsentence. "Whose phone is that?"

She reached for the SD-6 cell phone, but Sydney snatched it away, tucking it into her shorts pocket.

"Mine."

"Your phone is blue. That one's black."

Sydney forced a laugh. "Can't slip anything by you, Sherlock. Tell Scotland Yard I got a new one."

"Is it the same number?"

"Yes." Sydney still had her personal cell phone, and that was the only number she wanted Francie to have.

"Then it shouldn't work here. Right? I mean, what kind of calling plan is that?"

Sydney hoped her smile looked incredulous, because Francie's questions were making her nervous.

"Nationwide. Roaming. I don't know, Francie. It just works."

"I think it's kind of weird that you walked all the way down here just to make a phone call. Who were you calling, anyway?"

"Is there some point to this grilling?"

"I just don't know why you can't tell me where you're going, for once. Why do I have to play detective just to find out what you're doing?"

"You don't," Sydney said sharply.

"Then how come every time I turn around, you've taken off again? Why can't we hang out together?"

"Francie, weren't we just together all day?"

Francie hesitated, chewing her bottom lip. At last she gave a reluctant nod. "I just . . . I don't know. The other girls are okay. But it's not the same when they're around. It's not like . . . you and me." She sighed, her brown eyes beseeching. "Do I sound like the world's biggest loser?"

"No!" Sydney touched her friend's arm reassuringly.

"So . . . who were you calling?" Francie asked again.

"Just—I heard there was a cool dinner show downtown. And I was sitting here wondering what we were going to do tonight, so I thought I'd see how much tickets cost."

"How much?"

Sydney named a figure she hoped was in the ballpark. Francie's eyes rolled.

"You've got to be kidding! That bus trip today left me down to my last hundred bucks. If Roxy comes up with one more 'one last' thing we have to pay for, I'm going to be living on taro chips. And frankly, I'm getting kind of sick of those."

Sydney laughed. "How about a hot dog and an early movie, then? My treat."

"Just the two of us?" Francie asked hopefully.

Too late Sydney realized that if she was at a movie with Francie, she couldn't keep an eye on Ashley.

On the positive side, Ashley can't make a play for the prototype in a crowded theater, either.

"Yes," Sydney promised. "Just you and me."

* * *

About half the AKX sisters were having a nighttime swim in the hotel pool when Sydney and Francie returned from the movie theater. To Sydney's surprise, Ashley was among them, stroking the length of the pool in her pink bikini, so thin that every rib showed.

"I'm surprised she got her hair wet," Francie whispered, following Sydney's gaze. "She'll be up all night now, fixing that perfect 'do.'"

"By herself?" Sydney whispered back. "I thought it took a team."

Francie chuckled. "You want to go in? The water looks nice."

It did, but Sydney couldn't swim with her backpack on, and she wasn't about to leave it on a chair while Ashley was around.

"I'd rather just sit here and watch you," she replied. "Maybe drink something out of a coconut."

"Lazy!" Francie teased.

"You've got that right. Are you going up to change?"

"Yeah, but I'll hurry."

"If you see one of those hot hula guys on your way through the lobby, ask him if he can come out here and fan me. Maybe feed me some grapes . . . that type of thing."

Francie shook her head, a big grin on her face. "You've got Hawaii confused with Rome."

"I'm not confused," Sydney said, grinning back.

Francie left to put on her bathing suit. Sydney found a lounge chair, her eyes returning to the swimmers. Ashley had reached the far end of the pool, where she executed a perfect kick turn and began swimming directly toward Sydney. The girl had a good stroke, but that was no surprise. As Sydney watched, Ashley reached the shallow end, pulled her feet beneath her, and stood up, water streaming from her slicked-back hair. She wiped the chlorine from her eyes and opened them to find Sydney sitting just feet away, watching her.

Ashley's body stiffened. Hatred flickered into her eyes before she regained control of her haughty expression. Turning back toward the deep end with a twisting half dive, she swam off again, disappearing beneath the artificial waterfall.

"Hey! What's up?" Keisha asked, dropping onto the lounge chair next to Sydney's. "Who knew Hawaii could be so boring?"

Sydney smiled. "Why aren't you swimming?"

"Again?" Keisha looked pained. "There's way too much water here. I don't know why we couldn't have gone to Vegas. That's in the middle of nowhere too, but at least they have gambling."

"I'm not much of a gambler."

"You're breathing, aren't you?" Keisha stretched to emphasize her ennui. *"Life* is a gamble."

My life is, anyway, Sydney realized, glancing toward the waterfall again. Ashley still hadn't emerged from behind it.

"Tomorrow night, we all ought to go to a club," Keisha said. "There's got to be someplace around here that doesn't roll up its sidewalk at ten."

"Uh-huh," Sydney said distractedly.

How big could the area behind the waterfall be? Ashley had been back there long enough to call for room service.

"I'm going to go find Roxy," Keisha announced, standing up. "She's always good for a laugh."

"Okay. See ya."

Sydney waved as Keisha walked off—still no sign of Ashley. A dull buzzing sensation began in the pit of her stomach.

Is she even still back there?

There was nothing sly about sneaking off right under Sydney's nose. On the other hand, Ashley had already proven she was plenty sly. The buzzing in Sydney's gut turned into a full-fledged alarm. She rose from her chair and walked to the deep end, where she found a short tunnel leading behind the waterfall. Her heart in her throat, Sydney ducked through the tunnel. Above her head, a sheet of smooth water spilled from a rocky ledge into the swimming pool. She was standing in the sheltered spot beneath the falls, looking at the deserted back end of the pool.

Ashley had disappeared.

Running back out, Sydney looked all around the pool deck but saw no sign of the other spy. Half of her was desperate to find Ashley and learn what she was up to. The other half urged caution; maybe this was a trap. Ashley could be trying to lure her away, to give herself a chance at the prototype in Sydney's backpack.

Sydney hesitated a moment longer, making sure no one was looking, then melted into the landscaping. She had a pretty good idea where Ashley had hidden her change of clothes the last time she'd left a sorority event. She couldn't resist at least checking there.

Moving quickly, keeping to the shadows, Sydney hurried to the side of the hotel where she'd seen Ashley emerge before. But this time, instead of waiting on the street side, Sydney crept along the heavily vegetated path from the pool, every nerve on alert for the slightest sign of an ambush.

A sudden rustle up ahead made her freeze, heart pounding. A row of hibiscus bushes close to the hotel wall had a sidewalk-width space between them and the building; the noise seemed to be coming from there. Easing her body behind a palm tree, Sydney waited.

She didn't have to wait long.

Within seconds, Ashley emerged from behind the bushes, dried and dressed in black. Her blond hair stood out against the darkness, then suddenly disappeared, as if a flame had been snuffed.

She just put on that hat again, Sydney realized. *I'll bet she has no clue that I'm out here!*

It appeared that Ashley was on another of her own clandestine missions.

And I'm right behind her.

Easing out of her hiding place, Sydney followed at a distance as Ashley made her way to the street. Near the same bus stop, she stepped into a dark doorway, disappearing from sight. Sydney hung back and waited, certain Ashley would get on the bus again. Sure enough, the moment the bus appeared, Ashley darted out of the doorway and up its stairs, taking off in a cloud of diesel. Sydney turned and ran for her rental car. She was pretty sure where Ashley was headed— and this time she intended to be there waiting.

The road in front of the old warehouse off Hotel Street was deserted, except for a skanky-looking drunk relieving himself in the gutter. Sydney cruised the block, then decided to park down the street, where her car wouldn't be noticed. Sneaking back along the alley to the warehouse, she discovered a broken window to spy through, but found the building completely dark inside. She waited with a growing sense of apprehension, afraid she'd been wrong about Ashley's destination. Maybe her enemy had been aware of her presence after all, throwing her off by pretending to take the bus; she could have gotten off at the first stop. Sydney was starting to despair when a beam of light flashed through the empty building, accompanied by footsteps.

She crouched lower at the window, her pulse thudding in her ears. A man was crossing the floor, but, as before, she could make out little more than baggy pants and a sweatshirt with its hood pulled tight. He walked to a packing crate near the center of the warehouse and set the flashlight down, pointed toward the front of the building. Minutes later, Ashley walked into its beam and stood blinking, one hand shading her eyes.

"Are you alone?" he rasped.

"Of course," Ashley snapped. "Do you have to shine that thing right at me?"

Her contact reached down and spun the flashlight ninety degrees, leaving them both in shadow.

"Do you have it?" Ashley asked.

"What do you think?"

They regarded each other a long, silent moment. Then the man reached under his sweatshirt and extracted a paper-wrapped parcel the size of a brick.

"You know the terms?" he asked. "Everything's clear?"

Ashley nodded.

He extended the package toward her, then stopped, his hand hovering between them. "This isn't the kind of thing you want to screw up."

"No kidding. You know my creds."

"Right." He handed her the package.

Ashley held it briefly in both hands, then slipped it into the tote bag on her arm. "I'll be in touch."

"I'll be waiting."

She hesitated, perhaps wanting to say something else, then turned abruptly and strode out of the building. Sydney watched her go, wondering whether to follow her or stay with her male counterpart.

Ashley's got the package.

The thought decided her instantly. Whatever was in that bundle, Sydney wanted to know about it.

Backing away from the building, she hurried toward the front of the warehouse, expecting Ashley to turn left and head toward Hotel Street, like last time. She was halfway up the alley when Ashley crossed its mouth mere yards in front of her, having unexpectedly turned right. Sydney froze, both shocked and exposed, but Ashley never looked her way. Ashley's attention seemed fixed on something down the block as she scurried past, a tight grip on her bag.

Daring to move again, Sydney cut through a hedge, edging forward until she could see down the street. Ashley was picking up speed, trotting toward a cab parked at the corner. She closed the last few steps and yanked its door open, leaping in back as if it had been waiting just for her.

It was, Sydney realized with a sinking feeling. Whatever Ashley was carrying was too valuable to risk walking down Hotel Street with. She must have called for the cab in advance, to make sure she'd clear the area fast after her pickup. Sydney watched helplessly as the taxi cruised off down the road. Then she bolted out of hiding and sprinted for her parked car.

The cab had traveled about four blocks when Sydney picked up its red rear lights, staying back as far as she could to avoid detection. After following for a mile, she turned down a side street, then quickly turned again, running parallel to the cab. She was taking a risk, glimpsing the vehicle only at intersections, but she was more afraid of being spotted as a tail. Besides, she was already pretty certain they were headed back to Waikiki.

A block from the hotel, the taxi pulled over and Ashley climbed out. Sydney parked her rental car in the first available space, spying from behind the wheel as Ashley paid the driver and walked away. She seemed more relaxed than in Chinatown. Her steps bounced as she headed down the block, and she took off her hat and shook out her hair. Sydney eased out of her car and followed cautiously. There wasn't a lot of cover in the sweeping hotel entry, and while she could make up a plausible lie to explain her presence there, Ashley wasn't likely to believe it.

Within sight of the lobby, Sydney had to walk in the open. There was no doorman at that late hour, but she could see a desk clerk as she neared the entrance. Ashley was standing at the bank of elevators, waiting. As Sydney watched, the elevator doors opened and Ashley stepped inside.

Sydney ran across the lobby and reached the elevators in time to see that Ashley was headed down.

Down?

All the guest rooms were on the upper floors. The only rooms below the lobby were meeting rooms, a ballroom, the spa facilities . . .

She's going to hand off that package right here!

Sydney sprinted for the staircase and ran down one floor, racing the elevator. When it didn't stop, she hit the stairs again, chasing it down another level. Ashley got off this time and headed straight for the hotel gym. Her room key opened the glass door to the darkened facility, where a few lonely stair-steppers kept company with a deserted line of treadmills. Passing the equipment without a glance, Ashley walked toward the locker room.

Now what? Sydney wondered.

Following Ashley into the gym was asking for trouble. But if she didn't, she might lose the girl—and whatever intel she was carrying—out some unknown exit. Throwing caution to the wind, Sydney dashed into the gym.

The locker room lights were off, the only illumination coming from a bright red exit sign. Sydney made out shower stalls along the wall, and several tall, parallel banks of lockers in the center of the room. Ashley was nowhere in sight, but Sydney heard faint noises from behind the last row of lockers. Easing forward, every nerve stretched, she made her way to the source of the noise and peeked around the corner, drawing her head back abruptly.

Ashley was standing in front of an open locker, stowing the tote bag inside it.

Creeping to the nearest shower stall, Sydney

took shelter inside its dark alcove. She heard the locker door clang shut, then rattle as Ashley tested the lock. For a full minute, there was silence. Then Ashley's footsteps sounded, heading back toward the equipment area. The gym door closed, a distant click, and Sydney slumped with relief. Whatever was in that package was as good as hers.

Coming out of cover, she headed straight for the back row of lockers. They were the sort that ate quarters until eventually releasing a key—and there was only one with a key missing. Shrugging off her backpack, Sydney removed an all-purpose lock pick and went to work on the keyhole. She had the door open in seconds.

Grabbing the tote bag excitedly, she reached inside and pulled out the paper-wrapped parcel, holding it close to her face. Her fingers went for a loose edge on the paper, peeling it back impatiently.

Wham!

The brutal blow to the back of her head collapsed Sydney instantly, blackness seeping across her vision as she slid to the cold tile floor. She tried to turn, to fight, to at least stay conscious. . . .

The last thing she saw before she passed out was a blurred halo of blond hair.

"NO, WILSON. IT'S EARLY," Sydney mumbled. "Let me sleep for once."

Her tongue felt too big for her mouth, and something hard pressed into her cheek. She tried to pull the blankets up over her head, to delay waking a few more minutes, but her hand closed on empty air.

Her brain jolted with sudden recollection. Adrenaline flooded her bloodstream, kick-starting her heart and snapping her eyes wide open. She was lying on the cold tile floor of the hotel gym, and according to her watch, she'd been there a long time.

"The prototype!" she gasped, sitting up abruptly.

The room tilted like a sinking ship. For a moment she thought she would vomit. Her head throbbed painfully, and when she touched it, she found a large, tender goose egg behind her right ear. The skin wasn't broken, though—no blood— and a few slow, measured breaths made the floor horizontal again. Sydney reached for her backpack and dragged it closer, afraid of what she'd find.

Her hand shook as she checked the pack's main compartment: sunscreen, dark glasses, a half-folded map, and—to her complete amazement— the prototype. The T-shirt she'd used to disguise the case was still wrapped tightly around it. The case itself remained unopened, its lock and seal intact.

How could Ashley have missed it?

Unless she was so concerned about getting her own intel to safety that she didn't stop to look . . .

Sydney glanced around, every movement making her head hammer. Above her, the locker door stood open. With a tremendous effort, she pushed to her knees, then slowly to her feet. The locker was empty.

The package was gone.

* * *

Another half hour passed before Sydney felt well enough to walk to the elevator. Even then, she staggered as the car began its lurching journey to the sixteenth floor. The hall was hushed and deserted, but Sydney didn't let that stop her. Out of more clever ideas, she made her way to Ashley's door and pounded with all her strength.

The door flew open in seconds, saving her the pain of kicking it in.

"Sydney!" Gretchen exclaimed, her panicked look changing to one of anger. She was wearing an inside-out robe over pink baby-dolls, a spot of orange zit cream caking on her forehead. "What do you think you're doing? Do you know what time it is?"

"I need to see Ashley," Sydney said, shoving her way into the room. One of the beds was a twisted mess of sheets and blankets; the other was perfectly made.

"Ashley's not here," said Gretchen, putting her hands on her hips. "And this may surprise you, but I was sleeping."

"I have to talk to her. Where did she go?"

Gretchen's eyes narrowed. "Have you been drinking?"

"A little." It seemed like as good an excuse as any. "I just . . . Could you tell me where she is, Gretchen? Please?"

Gretchen considered, then tossed her head and sat on the unmade bed. "Ashley went home."

"Home?" Sydney's head pounded painfully as she tried to understand.

"L.A.," said Gretchen. "Remember L.A.?"

"I don't get it. She just packed up and left for L.A.?"

"Somebody called her—some sort of family emergency. She said she had to go, and she did."

A cover story. Things were starting to make more sense.

"What kind of emergency?" Sydney knew she was dealing with a lie, but she still couldn't help hoping for a clue. "Is somebody sick?"

Gretchen shrugged. "She didn't say. Ashley's weird like that. Secretive. You know?"

"Yeah," said Sydney. "I know."

* * *

"I don't think you should go in the water," Francie said worriedly, reaching over from the beach towel next to Sydney's. "Not with that lump on your head."

"It's nothing," said Sydney, pushing her friend's hand away. "And we weren't going to tell anyone, remember?"

To explain her sudden disappearance from the pool the night before, Sydney had told Francie she'd gone to the beachside bar for one of those fruity drinks, met a guy who'd bought her something stronger, and walked into a lamppost. Francie hadn't known whether to be amazed or furious—until she'd felt the bump under Sydney's hair. Then it had been all Sydney could do to talk her out of a trip to the emergency room.

"Don't blame me if you die in your sleep," Francie had finally muttered, giving up.

But now, after a long, death-defying rest, Sydney felt much better. She'd put on her black bikini and gone out to the beach with the rest of the sisters, who had decided they couldn't leave the islands without at least *trying* to surf. It seemed everyone was there that afternoon.

Everyone but Ashley.

Sydney still couldn't believe that Ashley was really gone, but she'd given Roxy the same story about a family emergency—and when Roxy had repeated it to the other girls, no one else seemed to think anything of it.

"Hey, Sydney! Are you coming out?" Roxy called now, her voice carrying up the beach. "You can have this board."

The redhead stood dripping in the shallows, her arm around one of the rented surfboards. Crystal blue ripples lapped at her calves, making the calm sea look more like a giant bathtub than an ocean. A few of the other sisters were out far enough to paddle, laughing at their own inept attempts to catch the twelve-inch-high waves sliding in toward shore.

"The water feels fantastic!" Roxy added encouragingly. "You really ought to try it."

Sydney hesitated, one hand on the backpack at her side. But with Ashley out of the picture and the entire sorority on the beach, no one was going to steal the prototype. Tossing the free end of her towel up to cover her pack, she stood and stretched, digging her toes into the warm white sand.

"I might give it a go," she said. "If you promise not to laugh."

Roxy shook her head, her long hair shedding sparkling drops. "No deal," she said, chuckling. "Why should you get special treatment?"

"Do you want to try it, Francie?" Sydney asked.

Francie glared disapprovingly from her towel. "No."

Roxy dragged the wet surfboard up the beach and dropped it at Sydney's feet. "Your turn. I'm whipped."

Sydney was reaching to pick it up when the ring of a cell phone made her freeze. Her SD-6 phone was in her backpack.

"Oops! I think that's mine," said Roxy, restarting Sydney's heart. She retrieved a phone from her straw beach bag, holding it an inch from her wet ear. "Hello?"

"So, you're really going in?" Francie said to Sydney, taking advantage of the break. "I think you're crazy."

"Come on, Francie. If I were going to die of a concussion, it would have happened last night."

She had meant her remark to be funny, but Francie's scowl deepened. "I don't even know who you are lately."

Sydney cast a nervous glance at Roxy, but the sorority president had turned her back on them. "No. . . . That's crazy," Sydney heard her say in a low voice. "What's going to happen now?"

"Francie," Sydney said, trying not to whine. "Can we please forget about last night? We're only here for two more days. Can we please try to have fun?"

"You don't think I'm trying?" Francie snapped.

Sydney lowered her voice to a whisper. "Can we at least not argue here?"

Francie shrugged and looked away across the beach.

Roxy hung up the phone. "You're not going to believe this!" she cried, turning back to face them. Her eyes were huge, her face flushed pink with excitement.

"What?" Sydney asked, sensing something big.

"Ashley was arrested at the Honolulu airport this morning. She's in jail!"

Francie gasped with astonishment. "For what?"

"Smuggling drugs!" Roxy reported breathlessly. "Can you even believe it?"

No, thought Sydney. *I can't.*

SYDNEY SPED TOWARD THE jail in her rental car, still reeling from the news of Ashley's arrest. It seemed impossible that this wasn't just another cover story—but it was one that didn't make any sense. Why would Ashley ruin herself within the sorority? Unless she had no intention of ever coming back . . .

Because she can't come back now, Sydney thought. *Not after this.*

Whatever else might happen, Ashley's days in Alpha Kappa Chi were over.

"I knew it!" Keisha had exclaimed as soon as all the sisters were gathered to hear the story.

They'd stood in a tight little group, dripping on the warm sand and staring wide-eyed at one another.

"You did not," Roxy had protested.

"Okay. I didn't know that *exactly,*" Keisha had admitted. "But there was always something wrong with that girl. She was never really one of us."

"You're right," Katie had agreed. "Not Alpha material."

A murmur of consensus had run through the girls, most of whom had seemed more titillated than shocked by Ashley's spectacular fall.

"But wait until people at school hear this!" Kira had said worriedly.

"Oh, wow!" Lee Ann had moaned. "That's going to be ugly."

Even Gretchen, Ashley's supposed friend, had shaken her head with the rest. "I always said there was something weird about that girl. I mean, not that she and I were ever very close."

"The main thing now," Roxy had finally broken in, "is damage control. Ashley did what she did, and she has to live with that. It's up to us to make sure she doesn't drag the sisterhood down with her."

Her pronouncement had been met with frantic finger snapping, signaling agreement. People had started shouting out so many ideas for polishing the AKX image that Sydney had gotten the impression the girls were kind of looking forward to the scandal.

"Is it just me?" Francie had whispered, pulling Sydney to one side. "Or do they seem . . . happy?"

"It's definitely not breaking anyone's heart," Sydney had whispered back. "I guess I wasn't the only one who didn't much like Ashley."

"But she's their *sister*," Francie had said, upset. "I mean, they let her pledge. They initiated her. Doesn't that mean anything? We don't even know her side of the story!"

Sydney had nodded. "I see what you're saying."

If the sisters didn't support Ashley, there was no reason to believe they'd ever stick by Francie. Or Sydney.

"I'll tell you what," Sydney had whispered, seizing the opportunity. "I'm going to cut out of here. I'll say I have a headache or something and catch a cab over to the jail. Just to see if it's really true, or if Ashley needs our help."

She had expected Francie to argue, but her friend had seemed relieved. "I'll go with you."

"No," Sydney had said quickly. "Stay here and back up my headache story. The way everyone's acting right now, I'd rather they don't know where I'm going."

"But it's not right. Why not send Gretchen? Or Roxy?"

Sydney had shrugged. "Ashley and I . . . at least

we're honest with each other. I just want to know what's really going on."

"When will you be back?"

"I have no idea. But it could be late, all right? Will you promise not to panic?"

Francie had smiled. "You really *are* a good friend. Do you know that?"

At least Francie preapproved my alibi this time, Sydney thought, driving the last mile to the jail.

After that, it had been a simple matter to sneak up to her hotel room, change into jeans and running shoes, and hide the prototype inside the potted silk orchid by the window. She didn't feel totally safe about leaving it behind, but that option seemed smarter than carrying it through jail security. Besides, with the case tucked down inside the big pot and the fake plant and moss replaced perfectly, no one but a pro would ever find it. Even if the call to Roxy had been faked and Ashley wasn't really in jail, it didn't seem likely that she'd venture back to the hotel.

Sydney parked the car and walked into the police station, ready to hear that Ashley had never been there. But she was. And after a lot of fast-talking, Sydney was taken to her cell.

"Ashley?"

It was shocking to see the girl on the other side of the bars. Ashley sat on the edge of a hard metal bunk, her pale skin sallow. Her head was in her hands, her hair an uncombed mess, and when she lifted her tear-streaked face, Sydney realized for the first time how much makeup she usually wore. She looked so much younger, scrubbed clean like that. Young and vulnerable.

"You must be happy," she greeted Sydney in a choked voice. Her tone was shaky but not surprised, as if she'd anticipated Sydney's arrival. "Come to gloat?"

"Actually, I'm kind of stunned you're here. Roxy told everyone you were busted for smuggling drugs."

"Yeah, I'll bet you were real amazed," Ashley said sarcastically, turning her face away. "Probably could have knocked you down with a feather."

But Sydney ignored the comment, hearing something besides the words.

"I *knew* you had an accent!" she said, trying to place the new twang in Ashley's voice. "That snotty Bel Air thing you do? I never bought it. You'd better tell your handler you need more work."

Ashley looked Sydney's way again, her expression incredulous. "My handler?"

"Or whoever coaches you in accents. Because I have to tell you, yours sucks."

"Great." Ashley's eyes welled up with tears and this time she didn't try to hide them. "What difference does it make now anyway? No one's ever going to talk to me again. I'm out of AKX forever. I'll probably have to change schools."

"Huh?" That seemed like the least of her problems to Sydney.

"You're right," Ashley said bitterly, her accent unraveling further, into something from a poverty-stricken region of the South. "By the time I get out of prison, everyone who knows me will have already graduated."

Sydney leaned against the bars, nonplussed. The way Ashley was carrying on was the last thing she'd expected. She was talking too much, for one thing—even a rookie spy knew to keep her mouth shut and wait for her agency to sort things out. On the other hand, she'd seen Ashley's acting before. Was the girl still working some sort of scheme?

"Let's be honest," said Sydney. "Graduating was never really your goal."

Ashley shot her a look of pure loathing. "I'm just poor white trash to you, aren't I?"

Sydney didn't answer, amazed.

"You're just like all the rest, judging a girl for the things she can't help. So what if I sold drugs? I never wanted to. When your momma's living off her 'boyfriends' and your daddy's as worthless as mine, *then* you can judge me. How else was I going to pay for college? How else could I have *ever* joined the Alphas?"

Ashley dashed her tears away and shook her head defiantly. "I don't care. Whatever they do to me now . . . at least I was somebody once. I was Ashley Evans, and believe me, that's a helluva lot better than Claralee Barker."

Sydney needed to sit down, but there wasn't a chair. She gripped the bars harder, to steady herself.

"You changed your name?"

"Like you didn't already know that," Ashley sneered. "I changed everything. Every little thing money could buy. My name, where I came from, how I looked, the way I talked . . ."

The defiance suddenly left her, and she broke down in ragged sobs. "I couldn't change who I was, though. I guess I'm stuck with that."

"So that package you had last night . . . ," Sydney ventured after a minute.

"Would have kept me in cash for months. And all I had to do was mule it back to L.A. No more nickel-and-dime calls in the middle of the night. No more hanging out in—" Ashley cut herself off abruptly. "Shouldn't I have an attorney?"

"Not to talk to me."

"Oh, right. Because *you're* not going to tell anyone." Ashley managed a cynical smile. "Whatever. You're just doing your job."

"My job?"

"Listen, there's one thing I do want to say." Ashley's voice shook. "I'm sorry I hit you on the head. I just . . . panicked. I never did anything like that before, and . . . you probably don't believe me, but I'm not a violent person. Sometimes people just have to . . ."

Her head went back into her hands. "Whatever," she repeated.

She seemed stripped bare, devoid of all hope.

"If this is the apology part of the program, what about what you did to me on the boat?" Sydney asked.

"You mean when I said Francie fell overboard?" Ashley raised her face wearily. "I was drunk. I really thought she did."

Sydney had been referring to the attack on the *Eagle,* but now she forgot that, distracted. "You . . . you did?"

"It's not impossible," Ashley said defensively. "There was a big splash. Roxy heard it too. In fact, she's the one who asked me if someone was missing."

Ashley sighed heavily. "I'm going to miss her most of all. Roxy was always so nice. I mean . . . a few things she said, I think she probably knew, but she never came out and accused me. Not like Jen, who was always threatening to turn me in if I didn't stop. She tried to act *so* understanding, but she didn't understand a thing. How could she? A few of us went to her parents' house once—heart-stoppingly, mind-numbingly rich. And Jen took it all for granted. You could tell she'd had everything she'd ever wanted since the very first day she was—"

"Wait. Jen knew you were selling drugs?"

Ashley shrugged.

"So you killed her." Sydney's voice came out flat, an accusation.

"What? No!" Ashley's horror seemed genuine. "God, no. Jen died of an asthma attack."

"But you wanted her dead," Sydney said, less certainly.

"You're crazy!"

She was starting to feel crazy. Nothing fit.

"I'm not talking to you anymore," Ashley announced, her old haughtiness returning. "It's one thing to be a narc, but if you're going to accuse me of murder . . ."

"You think I'm a *narc*?"

Ashley laughed bitterly. "It's a little late to play innocent. Besides, you're not going to catch anyone else in AKX. No one else is dealing, and if they were, Roxy would have warned them too."

"Roxy . . . Roxy warned you about me?" Sydney felt like she was working a puzzle without the box top. "About me being a narc?"

Ashley smiled, a little smugly. "Maybe she liked me more than y'all thought. Or maybe she didn't like you as much. You really thought she was your new best friend, didn't you? Let me tell you something: Roxy's smarter than that."

The truth slammed into Sydney's brain, obliterating everything else.

Roxy.

No.

Roxy!

If Ashley was truly only a small-time poser, that meant someone dangerous was still in the sorority. Someone Sydney had never suspected.

Roxy's the one who put me on to Ashley's disappearing acts. She's been pitting us against each other right from the start.

And Roxy's the one who invited me to pledge. If she . . . if she killed Jen . . . she'd be watching for someone like me to turn up.

Still, if she's been on to me all this time . . . That was Roxy on the Eagle!

"I have to go," Sydney blurted out, turning away from the bars.

Roxy had played her like a pro—and she'd never suspected it for a second. The funny, outgoing redhead had completely won her over. Won her friendship, her confidence, her trust . . .

And I left the prototype at the hotel!

* * *

Sydney sprinted down the hallway to her hotel room, expecting to see it destroyed again. More of the puzzle was becoming clear to her every second. She was now certain it was Roxy who had searched her room, timing her act so Ashley got the blame.

And I went running to her about it! Sydney felt sick as she remembered Roxy's wide-eyed attempt to involve hotel security. *She knew I wouldn't want that. She knew everything!*

Sydney fumbled with her room key, her hands shaking. She threw her door open, prepared for the worst.

Everything was exactly as she'd left it.

Huh?

She stood paralyzed in the doorway, unable to understand. Why hadn't Roxy gone for the prototype?

Stumbling forward, she scanned the room, searching for any sign of tampering. Nothing seemed to have been disturbed. Crossing to the potted orchid, she yanked up its silk flowers.

The prototype was gone.

She did it. It's Roxy.

Only a well-trained spy could search a room without leaving a trace. If Sydney hadn't spoken to Ashley, if she hadn't figured out what was going on, she might not have noticed the loss for hours— more than enough time for Roxy to meet her contact and hand off the device. The whole thing would have been over before Sydney ever suspected her. She might *never* have suspected her. . . .

Dropping the orchid, Sydney ran to the elevator,

then charged into the staircase when the car didn't appear. She hurtled down the sixteen flights, bursting into the lobby with a wild look on her face. She found Keisha on the outdoor terrace, flirting with some guy.

"Keisha!" she exclaimed, breaking into their conversation. "Where's Roxy?"

Keisha pointed back through the lobby, toward the front of the hotel. "She left to go shopping fifteen minutes ago. What's the matter with *you*?"

Not pausing to answer, Sydney raced through the lobby, out to the street in front of the hotel, and looked frantically up and down.

Roxy had the prototype and a fifteen-minute head start.

And Roxy had disappeared.

CLOTHES FLEW IN ALL directions as Sydney attacked Roxy's hotel-room closet. There was no attempt at subtlety in this last-ditch search effort—desperation drove her every move. Crazed by the realization that she had lost a nuclear prototype to an unknown enemy, she had broken into Roxy's room without even trying to be sly. Only luck had kept people out of the hallway while she was picking the lock.

Abandoning the closet, Sydney yanked open the top drawer of the dresser. All Roxy's clothes had been left behind, suggesting she fully expected to return. The first drawer was crammed full of bathing suits; the middle one held shorts and tank tops. And in the bottom drawer, behind the pajamas and sweatpants, was a shoulder-length blond wig. Sydney lifted it out for a closer look, grimacing as another mystery was solved.

It was Roxy I chased that night at Pearl Harbor! She must have worn this whenever she spied on me, so if I happened to spot her I'd think she was Ashley.

Sydney tossed the wig away in disgust. The ploy had worked perfectly. After all her specialized training, she had still let her personal dislike of Ashley completely cloud her vision. Worse, she had trusted Roxy simply because she was nice.

Because she seemed *nice,* Sydney corrected herself, still coming to terms with the realization that she didn't know the first thing about the girl.

Leaving the dresser, she ripped the bed apart, then checked the drapes, the bathroom, the wastebaskets. She didn't even know what she was looking for. Just anything, any little clue that might tell her where Roxy had gone . . .

A hotel pen rested on a pad beside the phone. Sydney tore off the top sheet of paper and ran with it to the window, looking for impressions created by writing on the missing upper sheets. Among the doodles and curlicues, she made out seven numbers.

A telephone number!

There was no guarantee it had anything to do with Roxy, but it was the only clue she had. Heart hammering, she took her SD-6 phone from her backpack and dialed.

"Oahu Helicopter Charters," a woman chirped on the answering end.

"Yes . . . I, uh . . . What kind of business are you?" Sydney blurted out. "I mean, do you rent helicopters? For people to fly by themselves?"

"We charter to licensed pilots who meet our other criteria." The woman's voice said plainly how unlikely she thought Sydney was to be in that group.

"Right." Sydney scrambled for the pen. "Can you tell me how to get there?"

* * *

Sydney drove like a maniac through cane and pineapple fields, down the final stretch of dirt road to the helicopter charter business. Red dust spewed from her tires as she screeched into the parking lot in front of the low metal building, but her eyes were glued to the tarmac, where the main rotor blades of a two-seater aircraft had just begun to spin.

A pilot sat at the controls, her distinctive red hair visible through the helicopter's back window. Braking in a long, gravel-crunching slide, Sydney leaped out of her car and sprinted across the tarmac just as the craft's horizontal landing skids began to lift.

The copter was eight feet off the ground before Sydney was close enough to jump. She launched herself full tilt, praying she'd be able to hang on as her hands closed around the skid on the empty passenger side.

The aircraft rocked, upset by the sudden change of weight. Sydney dangled like a rag doll, nearly losing her grip. Somehow she kicked her feet up and managed to swing a leg over the skid of the rapidly ascending copter. Clinging desperately, she pulled herself into a crouching position against one of the upright skid supports.

Don't look down, she told herself, dizzy with fear. The horizon reeled. Her stomach lurched. She couldn't believe what she'd just done. From her new perspective, the copter seemed to hover in place while the green fields fell away from her, spinning as they went.

Stop looking!

Mustering her courage, she inched her hand toward the passenger door. She couldn't reach the handle. Easing herself up straighter, she pressed her torso tight against the slick metal body of the craft. For the first time, her head came up to the window, allowing her to see inside.

Roxy was looking right at her. The two of them locked eyes through the glass. Sydney had only a moment to think how completely changed her former friend looked. Then Roxy smiled and pushed a lever, sending the copter into a terrifying dive.

Sydney's legs buckled beneath her, resuming their desperate crouch. Roxy was climbing again, banking to the left. Sydney knew only enough about helicopters to be certain of two things: There were limits to how radically they could be maneuvered, and Roxy wanted her to fall to her death.

The copter banked right and gained speed. Far below, the fields gave way to buildings. Roxy was headed toward the shoreline. She dipped, then climbed, then dipped again, every sudden change of direction testing Sydney's grip. Sydney held on with all her strength, and after a few more rapid maneuvers, Roxy leveled out and accelerated straight toward the ocean. Sydney couldn't help looking down again as a coral sand beach flashed by beneath her. She didn't even want to guess how high up she was now—or how fast Roxy was flying.

The sand gave way to sea, its blue growing darker as the water got deeper. Sydney clung to her skid, any thought of reaching for the door again completely forgotten. The sun was dropping toward the ocean in a rapidly accelerating arc. If she fell off now, she could be swimming all night.

Assuming I survive the fall, she thought, glancing down again. *That's probably assuming too much.*

About a mile off Koko Head, Roxy turned left and began flying parallel to the coast, east around the southern tip of the island. Sydney held on tight, her fingers numb with cold and strain. Wind whipped loose strands of her ponytail across her face and forced horizontal tears from the corners of her eyes. As the sun continued sinking behind her, she blocked out her fear and pain by trying to guess where Roxy was heading.

Southeast of Oahu lay a cluster of other Hawaiian islands: Molokai, Lanai, Maui, and little Kahoolawe. Sydney didn't think she could hold on long enough to land on one of them, but every minute she became more certain that wasn't their destination anyway. Roxy had continued to follow the shoreline and was now flying almost due north.

A rendezvous with a ship of some sort seemed like a possibility. It would have to be a big ship, though, to have a helipad, and Sydney didn't relish her chances against the number of enemy agents likely to be aboard. Her SD-6 phone was in her backpack; for a moment she actually considered getting it out and calling Wilson for help.

Except that he won't be able to do anything.

And she didn't dare loosen even one finger from her hold on the copter.

All of a sudden, the aircraft banked left, losing altitude. And there, up ahead, a forbidding little island pushed its rocky peak above the waves, nearly a mile offshore of Oahu.

She's going to land there!

The thought made Sydney's heart race. If getting onto a moving helicopter had been tricky, getting off one was sure to be worse. Roxy was coming down sharply and much too fast. If Sydney didn't bail out at just the right instant, she stood a good chance of being squashed like a bug. The bare soil of the tiny island rushed up to meet her, red and desolate. There were no trees, no flowers, no grass.

No matter when she jumped, it was going to be a hard landing.

Steeling herself for the worst, Sydney prepared to leap. Her survival instinct told her to do it at the first opportunity, even if it meant breaking a leg, but her training cautioned her to wait. If she jumped too early, Roxy could simply take off again, leaving her stranded with no way to follow. She had to be certain the aircraft was really going to land.

Her conflicting impulses in chaos, Sydney waited. The helicopter seemed to stop moving while the ground rushed up, up, up. She didn't dare try to turn around, which meant she was going to have to jump down between the skids, underneath the copter. If Roxy kept descending at her current crash velocity, there was no guarantee Sydney would be able to roll out of the area without being crushed. She balanced her weight on her toes, choosing her spot on the approaching ground. Breathing, breathing . . .

Now!

Six feet above the ground, Sydney sprang off the skid. Her running shoes twisted in the uneven lava, the impact jarring her legs. She fell forward onto her hands and knees as the copter slammed down above her, its skids crunching into the rocky soil on both sides. The whirring rotor blades overhead stirred up a choking, stinging storm of dust. Cramped and dizzy from her ride on the skid, Sydney forced her legs to move, to carry her out from under the copter to the door on its left-hand side. She was reaching for the handle when the door flew open.

Sydney staggered backward as Roxy jumped from the cockpit, landing in a fighting stance under the spinning rotor. She was wearing a tight blue tank and black jeans, a backpack over her shoulders. The gust from the blades whipped her loose hair into a cloud, but Roxy's eyes never wavered as she waited for Sydney to make the first move.

"I don't want to fight you, Roxy," Sydney

yelled, her words ripped away on the wind. "Just give me back what you took."

"The nuclear prototype?" Roxy laughed. "I don't think so. *Sister.*"

The word was a sneer, something dirty in Roxy's mouth. Sydney was facing a total stranger. Which made what she had to do a little easier.

Attacking in a rush, she threw a flurry of punches and kicks, but nothing found its target. Her punches were blocked; her kicks met air.

And then it was Roxy's turn.

Charging while Sydney was still off balance, she delivered a searing chop to the back of the neck. Sydney wheeled around only to catch Roxy's foot in her gut. The blow bent Sydney double. She was gasping for breath as Roxy charged again, grabbing her under the arms. With amazing strength, she lifted Sydney off her feet, up toward the dangerously spinning blades.

She's trying to kill me! Sydney realized. To fight for the prototype was one thing, but she'd never expected to fight for her life.

Ducking, Sydney jabbed Roxy's eyes. The girl released her so abruptly that Sydney fell into the dirt. Before she could get to her feet again, Roxy took off running.

Sydney scrambled up and gave chase, her shoes slipping wildly as she pursued Roxy down a slope of loose volcanic rock. Far below, she could see the ocean, gray in the failing light. Roxy was picking up speed, jumping from rock to rock on her way down to the shore. A long, curving finger of basalt stretched out into the ocean, creating a natural breakwater. Roxy flung herself down the last bit of hill onto its landward end, running seaward along its spine. And that was when Sydney spotted the empty gray Zodiac bobbing in the shadow of the rocky ledge. The boat was moored and waiting, and Roxy was headed straight for it.

Sydney made the punishing jump behind Roxy, forcing her wobbly legs into a sprint despite the uncertain surface beneath her feet. Roxy reached the boat first and grabbed its mooring line, pulling it close enough to board. Inflatable pontoons on the sides of the open fourteen-foot boat met in a V at its bow; its flat stern was dominated by an enormous outboard engine. Swinging a leg over the nearest pontoon, Roxy tumbled from stable land into the rising and falling boat, then quickly released the line, freeing the vessel. A swift current carried it away from the rocks as Roxy turned to start the engine. Still running full tilt, Sydney jumped, landing in a heap on the boat's hard bottom.

The sudden change in weight nearly capsized the light craft. Roxy staggered, clutching the outboard for support. Pushing up to her knees, Sydney found a wooden oar tucked under the edge of the nearest pontoon. She grabbed it and lurched to her feet, jabbing the handle hard into Roxy's kidneys. Roxy gasped with pain. Letting go of the engine, she assumed a wobbly fighting stance. Sydney swung the oar around like a martial-arts weapon, aiming the flat of the blade at Roxy's head.

The blow connected with a sickening crack. Sydney's stomach clenched as the vibrations traveled up the wooden handle into her hands. For a fraction of a second, the antagonism left Roxy's blue eyes, and they stared in wonder. Then they rolled up into her head and she fell forward into Sydney's arms.

Tears streamed down Sydney's cheeks as she laid her former sister in the bottom of the boat and checked for a pulse. To her relief, Roxy was still alive. A moment later, the girl groaned and moved her head slightly. She wouldn't be down for long.

Crawling forward, Sydney found a spare dock line. She tied Roxy's hands and feet before tethering the free end of the line to a ring on the floorboards. Then, almost afraid to hope, she unzipped Roxy's backpack and looked inside.

The prototype was there. So was Sydney's GPS unit.

"You broke into my car, too?" Sydney demanded, outraged.

Roxy moaned, but Sydney could have sworn a hint of a smile played around the girl's lips. Taking her SD-6 phone from her backpack, Sydney dialed Wilson.

"I've got the prototype," she reported.

"Yes. I know."

"Oh. Right." As far as Wilson knew, she'd had it all along. "I need to get rid of it now. And of something else, too. Is your boat here yet?"

"It's just outside Honolulu Harbor. I was going to call you when they docked."

"Tell them not to dock. They need to meet me at sea."

"Sydney, what's going on?"

Roxy sat up abruptly, leveling a malevolent gaze at Sydney.

"Things are, um . . . complicated," said Sydney. "Can I explain later?"

"Just tell me this: Is there a problem?"

"Not unless you consider having an enemy agent tied up on the floor of a rowboat a problem."

"That's my girl!" Wilson said. "All right, here's what we'll do. Do you have your GPS unit?"

"Yes."

The two of them set coordinates for a rendezvous at sea, where Roxy could be transferred secretly.

"And Sydney?" Wilson added before she hung up. "Good job. I'm proud of you."

"Thanks."

But the praise didn't mean as much as it once would have. And the gathering darkness didn't prevent her from seeing the girl she'd believed was her friend huddled in the bottom of the boat.

Sydney found the start cord on the engine and pulled it savagely, jerking the motor to life.

Then, with a watchful eye on Roxy, she wheeled the boat around and roared off into the open ocean.

15

STARS WERE TWINKLING OVERHEAD when the SD-6 yacht pulled into Honolulu Harbor, but Sydney didn't see them. She and two senior SD-6 agents were down below in a soundproof cabin, questioning a surly Roxy.

"We know you're K-Directorate," said Agent Ramirez, an older intelligence officer with graying streaks in her black hair. She'd told Sydney that her specialties were psychology and interrogation, but so far those skills weren't much in evidence.

"You don't know anything," Roxy replied, her smile thin and provoking.

"Then why don't you tell us?" Agent Warren cut in.

A huge, intimidating man, Warren looked more like a professional wrestler than an undercover agent. Sydney didn't want to guess what his specialty was, but the way he kept cracking his knuckles suggested some unpleasant possibilities.

"We're going to find out," he added. "One way or another."

"And bring me to justice, right?" Roxy sneered. "I'll save it for the judge."

"I *am* the judge. And these two here?" Warren indicated Sydney and Ramirez. "Consider them the jury."

Roxy laughed mockingly. "Those aren't *my* peers. Your junior there couldn't find her own butt with a magnifying glass."

Sydney bristled, but Warren only smiled.

"She found you, didn't she?" he taunted. "And she found the hardware. Twice. If she's that incompetent, what's your excuse?"

"She got lucky!" Roxy flung back, goaded.

The yacht jolted, then stopped. Ramirez checked her watch. "We're docking. And this conversation is going nowhere."

"Let me talk to her alone," Sydney urged her senior agents. "Just give us a few minutes."

"What are you going to do? Beat me up?" Roxy

was tied to a chair, unable to move her hands or feet, but her tone was supremely unconcerned. "I'm shaking in my boots."

Warren cracked his knuckles in Roxy's face. "Don't worry. Our methods are more efficient than that. Come on, Ramirez."

Motioning for the other agent to follow him out of the room, he pointed a finger at Sydney. "You have ten minutes. Then you're out of here, and I take over. By myself."

A trace of fear crossed Roxy's face as Warren closed the door, but the second she saw Sydney watching, her features reverted to her former condescending expression.

"So. Just me and Agent Bristow," Roxy said. "Or should I say Wannabe Agent Bristow?"

"I am a trainee. So what?" Sydney pulled her chair closer to Roxy's, until only a narrow gap remained between their knees. They glared at each other across the short distance as if they had never been friends.

We never were friends, Sydney reminded herself. *It was all a big lie.*

So how come looking at Roxy now made her want to cry?

"You killed Jen Williams," Sydney accused, choosing anger over tears.

Roxy's answering smile was so cold it raised

201 — SISTER SPY

the fine hairs on the back of Sydney's neck. "Jen was a little too smart for her own good."

"She caught on to you," Sydney guessed. "And once your cover was blown, you had no choice but to kill her."

"There's always a choice," Roxy said with a philosophical tilt of her head. "I tend to like the easy way."

A shudder rocked Sydney's body. The girl was a cold-blooded killer.

"So you snuck up on her while she was asleep, put a pillow over her face, and suffocated her," said Sydney, trying not to see the horrible scene in her head.

"Please!" Roxy sounded genuinely offended. "That's pretty crude, isn't it? Don't they have doctors where you work? People who can mix you up a little something?"

Sydney grimaced. Had it been an undetectable poison, then? Or maybe some other substance, one that caused an asthma-like reaction?

"The thing about Jen was, she should have seen it coming," Roxy continued. "She was only half as naïve as you are. I really doubt, for example, that Jen would have walked into a cocktail party and asked if a dead girl had been having trouble breathing. Way to go, Columbo. How do you think you got into AKX in the first place? It wasn't your fashion sense."

"So you knew," Sydney murmured, appalled by her own blindness. "All this time you only wanted me where you could watch—"

"And I'm *positive* that pushing a potted plant off a catamaran, then getting some drunk to say the splash was her best friend wouldn't have made our Jen drop cover in front of two hundred people."

"It was . . . You—you pushed off a plant?" Sydney sputtered.

"Big fake palm tree. I'm surprised no one missed it. Not even you." Roxy's smile was so smug that Sydney felt a sudden urge to slap her.

"And then you manipulated Ashley into thinking it was Francie."

"Manipulated!" Roxy hooted. "That's a two-dollar word for a nickel event. In case you haven't noticed, Ashley isn't the brains of any operation."

"Ashley likes you. In fact, she loves you. You could have helped her, but instead you just used her."

"Ashley!" Roxy spat the name. "Have you ever met anyone more pathetic? Losers like Ashley deserve what they get. She'd have ended up exactly where she is without any help from me."

"But you knew what she was up to. You could have set her straight."

Roxy looked disgusted. "What is Ashley to me? Or to you, for that matter? I've got to be honest—I don't see you going too far in this business."

"Not like your mommy and daddy, huh, Oxana?" Agent Warren asked, walking back into the room. He was waving a coded fax transmission, his expression jubilant.

Roxy's pale face drained to white.

"Funny thing about DNA," he continued. "We didn't have yours on file, but the computer took one look and kicked out profiles for both your parents. See, after their little 'accident,' we had plenty of time to collect samples."

"I'll kill you!" Roxy screamed, lunging forward. The unsecured chair fell over, leaving her struggling and shrieking on her side, desperately trying to get to Warren.

"You're with me," Ramirez said, grabbing Sydney by the arm and pulling her out of the cabin. "We need to shut this door."

The last thing Sydney saw was Roxy, spitting and gnashing her teeth, tears of rage wetting her twisted face.

"I just saw the X ray of Suler's case," Ramirez remarked conversationally. "Everything's inside and in perfect condition. Congratulations."

From behind the heavy door, Sydney heard another faint scream.

"Now we'll get the intel we want too," Ramirez

said, nodding toward the door. "It's always just a question of finding the right angle."

Sydney's entire body began trembling. "But . . . I don't understand."

Agent Ramirez nodded sympathetically and patted Sydney's shoulder. "Neither did we, until those results came through. I've still got Research chasing out the details, but it seems your friend's parents were both KGB, stationed in the United States. Oxana—Roxy—was born and raised here. When she was thirteen, her parents were killed in a joint mission, and after that we don't know yet."

"You think she's SVR?" The SVR, the Russian foreign intelligence service that supplanted the disbanded KGB, was a legitimate agency, not like the renegade branch of the Russian underground known as K-Directorate.

"Doubtful. But what an easy recruit for K-Directorate! Play on that pain and anger, convince her that the CIA shot two innocent people, offer her vengeance while telling her she's doing something great for her true homeland. . . ."

Ramirez's expression grew wistful, as if she'd have liked to have that job. "Piece of cake. I'm not kidding."

Sydney could see that she wasn't.

"I need some air," Sydney blurted out, overwhelmed.

"Why don't you get out of here? Head back to your hotel," Ramirez urged. "You couldn't have done a better job, but we'll take it from here."

Sydney stumbled up the ladder to the deck, barely acknowledging the crew or the other agents in her haste to get away. Even the cool night air couldn't cut the buzzing in her head as she jumped down to the dock and jogged off. An incredible pain had seized her, and all she knew for sure was that she needed to find someplace quiet. A place she could think. And recover.

And cry.

*　*　*

From the vantage point of the lighthouse, Sydney watched the SD-6 vessel putting back to sea. The hour was late and the yacht was running with minimal lights, but she was certain the craft nosing out of the harbor was the one carrying Roxy and the Suler prototype back to Los Angeles.

The knowledge brought her no joy. Everyone had told her what a great job she'd done on this mission, but even after a couple of hours of decompressing by herself, she still felt sick.

There was something wrong with a world where girls her own age could be in so much trouble. She wished she'd never gotten mixed up in any of it. Maybe Ashley and Roxy deserved whatever punishments they had coming . . . but why did she have to be involved?

Every time she closed her eyes she saw Ashley's broken, tear-streaked face and knew that things hadn't had to turn out that way. Not if someone had stepped in and cared . . .

And Roxy . . .

Her stomach twisted every time she imagined Roxy's life. She hadn't forgotten that Roxy killed Jen. But she also knew firsthand the pain of losing a mother. To have lost both parents, and lost them like *that* . . . No wonder Roxy had fallen in with K-Directorate. It was amazing her mind hadn't snapped.

Maybe SD-6 can help her, Sydney thought hopefully. *Rehabilitate her or something.*

But whether Roxy would be held in prison or somewhere more secluded, Sydney wasn't sure. The CIA was obviously going to want to learn as much as it could from her. Once Roxy was made to cooperate, she could be a gold mine of new information. Of course, gaining that cooperation was likely to take a while. . . .

Sydney sniffed back a headful of tears and wiped her wet eyes on her shirt.

Doing something good just shouldn't feel this bad.

Francie was probably frantic with wondering where she was, and by now even the other sisters had likely noticed her absence. The official SD-6 cover story to explain Roxy's disappearance was that she'd been arrested for dealing with Ashley. Wilson could make that happen on paper, and Roxy wouldn't be around to refute it. Still, the idea of going back to the hotel and floating that lie to AKX was too depressing to contemplate.

Doing *anything* with AKX was too depressing to contemplate.

"Sydney?" A quiet voice a few feet behind her made her spin around.

"Noah?"

"I want you to notice that I didn't sneak up this time," he said, moving closer. "At least, I tried not to."

"What are you doing here?" she asked incredulously. "Where did you come from?"

"I never left," he said. "I told you I had a few days off."

She couldn't believe he was really there. His presence seemed like a mirage, something her weary brain had invented to escape reality. She reached a hand toward him slowly, as if he were an image on the surface of a bubble.

"Tough night, huh?" he said sympathetically.

"How did you find me here?"

He shrugged. "I talk to people. I hear things. When the boat came in, I figured you'd be at the dock. You weren't, so I kept looking."

"I'm glad you did," she said, trying to swallow the lump in her throat. "I've been wanting to tell you . . . I'm sorry for the other night."

He waved the words away. "You were busy. I should have known better."

He took another step closer, close enough to see into her eyes. "I thought maybe now that your mission's over . . . But this doesn't look like a party."

"No." Sydney sniffed again, and before she could blink them back her tears overflowed. "Oh, Noah, I don't know what I'm doing anymore! Everything's so messed up."

She expected him to try to talk her out of it, to tell her what a great job she'd done, like everyone else. But instead, he opened his arms and folded her safely inside them.

"I feel that way four days out of five," he murmured into her hair. "It doesn't make you a bad person."

She started to laugh, but halfway up, the sound caught in her throat, turning into a sob. She wrapped her arms around him, squeezing hard as the tears continued to fall. He let her cry, just being there, just holding her. Somehow she knew he understood exactly how she felt.

How could I have ever considered replacing him with Burke? she wondered.

Burke was a nice guy, but he would never, ever know her the way Noah already did.

How can he, when I can't tell him anything?

To be in a relationship with someone who could never truly be part of her life seemed impossible now. She couldn't believe she'd seriously thought about it.

I wouldn't have, if Noah hadn't been so cold. If he hadn't acted like he didn't want anything to do with me . . .

It suddenly occurred to her he wasn't acting that way now. Stifling her tears, Sydney lifted her face up to his. The tender expression she surprised there took her breath away.

"Noah?"

"Yes?"

"I was wondering . . ."

His muscles tensed beneath her hands. She knew what he was thinking, that she was going to start making demands, ultimatums.

"I was wondering," she repeated, "if you could kiss me now."

His tension melted away. He lowered his face to hers. "Funny," he said huskily. "I was wondering the same thing."

Then their lips came together, hungry and hot,

and it was Paris all over again. The same storm swept through her, the same aching need. Her hands went into his hair and down his back, trying to memorize him. Her knees gave way. Her breath came in gasps. Noah was the one she wanted, the only one she'd ever wanted.

And when he lifted his mouth from hers and she looked into his eyes, everything she'd been thinking was mirrored right back to her. He couldn't deny it. He didn't even try.

He felt the same way.

16

"I'M WHIPPED," FRANCIE ANNOUNCED, dumping the crumpled contents of her suitcase onto her dorm room bed. "Who knew joining a sorority would be so exhausting?"

They had just returned from Oahu, the long flight and subsequent bus ride to campus as tense and sub-dued as the trip out had been exuberant. The sisters of Alpha Kappa Chi were in shock over the dual loss of Roxy and Ashley. No one had known what to say, so mostly they'd just kept quiet—except for poor Keisha, who had cried off and on the entire way home.

Sydney dumped out her own suitcase, then turned to face her friend.

"About the sorority, Francie," she said. "I can't go through with it. I didn't want to say this in front of the other girls, but after everything that's happened . . ."

"Oh, thank heavens!" Francie exclaimed, sitting down on her pile of laundry. "I've spent the past five hours trying to figure out how to tell you the same thing."

"You have?"

"I really expected to like it, but it was horrible! I was never going to fit in with those girls; they didn't want me in the first place. And it's not the money, because let's face it, the amount they have is unnatural by any human standard. It was their complete and total lack of interest in anything but themselves. If you didn't *wear* just the right thing, or *say* just the right thing, or *do* just the right thing . . . I feel like I've been to boot camp instead of Hawaii. And don't take this the wrong way, Syd, but they were really starting to change you."

Sydney smiled sheepishly. "I guess I should have known I wasn't sorority material."

"It wasn't you; it was *them*. If you had let *me* pick the house . . ." Francie brightened. "Maybe next fall we can—"

"Don't even think it!" Sydney interrupted, holding up her palm. "By next fall I plan to have forgotten any of this ever happened."

Not that she expected to succeed. It would be a

long, long time before she put her Hawaii mission behind her. To have been so wrong about two different girls had seriously rocked her faith in her own judgment. She didn't think she'd ever look at anyone in quite the same trusting way.

"So what are we doing tonight?" Francie asked.

"You mean besides laundry?"

"It's Friday night." Francie checked her watch. "And it's early. We ought to be able to come up with something better than laundry."

"What happened to being exhausted?"

Francie grinned playfully. "I think what I *said* was that being in a sorority is exhausting. Suddenly, I feel all better."

"I don't. I'm going to put my stuff away, go to bed early, and be ready to hit the books tomorrow."

"Wow. Thrilling. How will you stand the excitement?"

A sharp rap on the door made Sydney jump, then take a calming breath.

You're home, you're safe, you're just another college student, she reminded herself.

But it was getting harder to make the transition back to normal life. In fact, her job was starting to make her wonder if "normal" even existed. As far as she was concerned, the entire concept of normalcy was on trial.

"Get that!" Francie said. "You're closer."

Sydney walked to the door and pulled it open, only to find herself face to face with Burke, a huge, happy grin on his handsome face.

"Welcome back!" he said.

He pushed some daisies into her hands and kissed her on the cheek, a quarter-inch of strawberry stubble tickling her as he withdrew. She could tell by the way he smelled that he had recently showered and shampooed, but instead of being a turn-on, his fresh scent only reminded her how many hours she'd just spent traveling. He wasn't catching her at her best—or at her most prepared.

"Burke! What's going on?" she asked, shooting an amazed glance over her shoulder at Francie. "We didn't have plans, did we?"

"Nope," he said, pleased with himself. "I was so glad you were finally coming home that I decided to surprise you. I have reservations at the Velvet Vegan," he added, waggling his eyebrows. "And they don't give those to just anyone."

"Oh, no," said Sydney, laughing. "That's a *very* fancy dive."

Burke nodded smugly. "Romantic, too. I probably shouldn't tell you this, but I fully intend to sweep you off your feet."

Francie giggled.

Burke craned his neck around the door frame and waved at her. "Hey, Francie."

"Hey, Burke."

"You don't mind if I steal your roomie, do you? I'd invite you along, but frankly, you'd cramp my moves."

Sydney couldn't help laughing again. Burke was so refreshingly up-front.

"You're crazy!" she said, lightly slapping his arm. "And thanks for the flowers. But I'll have to take a rain check on dinner."

His face fell. "I should have called first, shouldn't I?"

"It's not that. It's just . . ."

How could she tell him what she'd decided in Hawaii? She needed a plan, a speech, a clear-cut way of ensuring they'd still be friends.

And whatever she came up with, she couldn't tell him about Noah. Francie didn't even know about Noah yet. Besides, there was nothing settled between them. They'd spent most of a night talking, walking around Honolulu together, but no one had said the *L* word. No one had mentioned the future. They were spies, after all, and that made the future an uncertain thing.

But there was something between them now. Something definite.

Cooling things off with Burke was the right decision.

Still . . .

He seemed so thrilled to see her. And it was

nice to have someone in her everyday life, some-one who truly cared. Someone smart, and funny, and . . . hot.

No. Do it now. Tell him now.

"It's just that I wasn't expecting to go to such a fancy restaurant tonight," she said, wimping out. "All of my evening gowns are at the cleaners."

"That *is* a dilemma." His grin crept back. "Where are your bikinis?"

"You'd like that, wouldn't you?"

"I get it. Trick question. Right?"

"Just go," Francie piped in. "You have to eat."

Burke offered Sydney his arm, bent at the elbow as if they were attending a formal function. He stood there expectantly, waiting for her to take it. . . .

And she did.

"See you later, Francie," she called as she walked out the door. "But not *too* much later," she cautioned Burke. "I have a lot to do tonight."

"You're right," he said, leading her down the hall. "After a splendid vegetarian repast, we're go-ing to an old film festival at a completely preten-tious art house I'll try to impress you with."

"I can't," she said, pulling away.

But Burke held on to her hand. *"Lawrence of Arabia,"* he wheedled. "Peter O'Toole with a tan. You *know* you want to."

And she did.

"Okay. But that's it—after the movie I'm coming straight home."

"Right. Immediately after we stop for coffee and ice cream."

"You're impossible!"

"I can be. But don't you kind of like it?"

"Maybe," she admitted.

I still have to tell him, though. I'll tell him at the restaurant. No, that will ruin the movie. I'll tell him after, at coffee.

She looked into his trusting hazel eyes, feeling terrible. Burke had never been anything but nice to her, whereas Noah . . .

I don't have to tell him tonight. I mean, I'll definitely tell him. Eventually.

"It's so good to have you back," he said. "It's probably not manly to admit this, but I really, really missed you."

"You did?"

"Every day." He stopped walking, as if a horrible thought had just struck him. "Wait a minute—is this the part where I'm supposed to act cool and detached? Because if it is, I want a do-over."

His grin was so infectious that Sydney grinned back, her heart thawing into a puddle.

Tonight, tomorrow, the next day . . . Is there really such a rush?

Noah was right when he called it a **bad idea** for agents to get involved in close relationships.

He said it isn't fair to the people we love, that a spy can **die** any day.

But Roxy taught me the real reason.

It's because we can't trust anyone.

Not anyone.

Not ever.